The Wrangler's Mail Order Bride

CINDY CALDWELL

By Cindy Caldwell:

Wild West Frontier Brides Series

The Chef's Mail Order Bride
The Wrangler's Mail Order Bride
The Bartender's Mail Order Bride
The Teacher's Mail Order Bride

Copyright © 2015 Cindy Caldwell
All rights reserved.
ISBN: 1517214920
ISBN-13: 9781517214920

This book would not exist without the help, wisdom, guidance and encouragement of Kirsten Osbourne and Ashley Merrick.
Thank you from the bottom of my heart.

Chapter One

Clara looked up at the gray, dreary sky and held out her hand, watching as the snowflakes settled on her palm. She wished she'd known it was going to bakery. She would have grabbed her winter hat, but this early spring snowstorm had come as a surprise.

To everybody, she guessed, as she closed the door of the bakery behind her and looked up to see the horses pulling the delivery wagon stomping their feet, their breath coming out in great bursts of white.

"Oh," she said under her breath as she looked around, wondering what had happened to the driver, and why he'd left the horses so long that they had clumps of snowflakes in their manes that were turning to ice. She imagined that the storm had caught them, too, with no time to put blankets on the horses to stave off the cold.

Pulling on her gloves, she walked to the two chestnut brown horses hitched up to the delivery wagon. As she approached the horses, they turned toward her, slowed their stomping and quieted. "There's a good horse," she said as she stroked their noses and patted their manes, pulling out as much ice as she could and tossing it to the ground.

When she'd gotten out as much ice as she could, she stroked their heads again. "It's too cold for you to be standing here. I'm going to look for your owner."

Their reins hung on a post at the side of the street and she spun in a circle, searching for the owner of the wagon. The wooden back was covered with a tarp, making it impossible to see what the items were that were being delivered. Clapping her hands together to keep warm, she walked to the back of the wagon and tried to lift up a corner of the tarp to see what was inside and maybe get a hint to where the driver might be. As she lifted the corner of the tarp and leaned down to peek under it, the cases of beer bottles flashed in the light and she stood quickly, taking a step back toward the wall. "All right. Beer. Now, where might that…"

She turned to her right. Light, music and loud voices spilled out from the saloon next to the bakery. She normally did her best to ignore it, as her brother, Robert, had specified that as a requirement for her to take the job at this bakery after her friend, Sadie, had closed the bakery she'd worked in since she was in school and had left for Arizona to get married.

She took a quick look back to the horses, one of them turning its ears in her direction. Breathing deeply, she walked over to the saloon, almost sure the horses' owner was inside. *If he is, he shouldn't be.* Heat rose in her cheeks as she hesitated outside the door, peering inside with the top of her bonnet pulled down. It wouldn't do for her to be recognized here.

Close to the door, men laughed, and she could make out a few of their words.

"Charlie, pour me another, would you? I've got a little time before I need to get this load of beer to the next stop," a man's voice said.

Her blood boiling now, she looked back at the

horses as they stomped their feet even harder and started to whinny, tugging at the reins that held them in place under the frosty onslaught of snow and ice.

Standing as tall as she could, she squared her shoulders and took a step toward the voice, hoping against hope that no one she knew would see her. But what choice did she have? Right was right, and it was *not* right to leave dependent animals out in the cold with no way for them to find shelter.

The brim of her bonnet covered her eyes as she strode to the sound of the man's voice she'd heard moments before. As she looked up, she stood in front of a tall, burly man leaning against the bar, a bottle of beer in his hand.

She cleared her throat and said, "Sir, are those your horses hitched to the delivery wagon out front?"

His eyes widened with surprise and he looked from Clara out the door and back to her, his chin jutting out as he folded his arms across his chest. "Maybe yes, maybe no. What's it to you, young lady?"

Her heart beat faster as she pulled back her

bonnet and looked up at him. "They are very cold, sir. Their manes are full of ice, although I removed what I could. It's snowing even harder now and they need to be sheltered, somewhere warm." Her face flushed as the words came out in a rush.

"Yeah, yeah, yeah. They're fine. Now run along home, little lady, while I finish my drink. I'll get to them right quick." He turned and winked to the man sitting next to him as he laughed.

"They are *not* fine, sir. This is…this is…just not right." Clara's fists clenched at her sides as she fumed. How could anyone be so…cruel?

The man burst into laughter again, nudging his friend with his elbow. "Now how do you know that? Did they tell you?"

Clara gasped, thinking yes, in some way, they did let her know they were freezing. "That's fine, sir. I'll just take care of it on my own," she said before turning on her heel and stalking out of the saloon.

As she marched down the stairs and toward the horses, all she could think of was that they needed to be warm. That they deserved to be taken care of.

She didn't exactly have a plan. Had no idea

where she would take the horses. All she knew was that she couldn't walk the short distance home and leave them there.

She didn't even look back at the saloon as she walked to the hitching post. "Don't you worry. We'll think of something. Maybe Robert will let you..."

"Hey! Hey! Take your hands off my horses."

She held her breath and turned toward the saloon door as the man she'd been talking to rushed down the stairs and ran in her direction.

She dropped the reins she'd been holding, saying to the horses as she quickly patted their noses, "It'll be all right now," before she turned and ran in the opposite direction, ducking behind the corner of the bakery she'd left not long before. She leaned against the wall until her breath evened out again and her heart stopped thudding in her chest.

She turned slowly and peeked around the corner to where the wagon was, hoping that the man hadn't seen where she'd gone, and breathed a sigh of relief as she saw that the man had retrieved his coat, untied the horses and was heading to his next destination or—she hoped—back to where the horses could get in out of the cold.

With a thought that she'd inquire about the deliveryman tomorrow when she went to work, she turned and headed toward home.

She took off her gloves and clapped them together outside on the stoop of the large house that she lived in with her brother, Robert, and his wife. She untied her bonnet, shaking the snow off of it as well, then turned, opened the door and set them down on the small table, shrugging off her coat and hanging it on the rack by the door.

"Clara, is that you?" her brother called from the living room.

She swung the big, oak door open and entered, kissing him and her sister-in-law, Margaret, on their cheeks. "Yes, it's me. I'm sorry I was a little late. I…"

"Had to help a stray kitten or puppy, I'm sure," Margaret said with a smile.

"Actually, it was a horse this time," Clara said, her heart full with hope that she'd actually been of help to the beautiful horses.

"A horse?" her brother said, his eyebrows

raised. "Well, that's a new twist, dear sister."

"You do have a way with animals." Margaret set her teacup down on the table beside her and leaned back onto the sofa, turning her eyes to Robert and clearing her throat.

"Oh, yes," he said as he blinked quickly and turned toward his wife. "Clara, there's something that Margaret and I need to speak with you about. Why don't you have a seat?"

Margaret patted the settee, encouraging Clara to come sit beside her. Clara had always been grateful to her brother and Margaret for taking her in when her parents had left Chicago to move to New York. She plopped down beside Margaret, her heart beating a little faster at the formality. Dinner was normally ready when she got home, and this was very different.

Margaret nodded to her husband, and Clara looked toward her brother and wondered why his cheeks were flushed.

"It has been wonderful to have you live here with us, Clara, and Margaret and I have enjoyed it greatly. It's been a wonderful opportunity for us to get to know you as the difference in our ages precluded that as we were growing up.

The ten-year age difference between them had resulted in them virtually being raised in different households. Robert had left for college when she was only eight years old, so she hadn't gotten to know him until recently, accepting his kind offer to live with them.

"As you know," he continued, "the banking world is ever-changing." He smiled at his wife, who nodded to him, encouraging him to continue.

"And as a banker, I am always prepared to serve my employer where most needed. And right now, I am most needed in New York," he finished quickly, reaching for his tea and sipping it as he looked at the ceiling.

"New York!" she cried, turning to Margaret.

Taking her hand, Margaret said, "Clara, I know it's a surprise. It was to us as well. But we want you to know that we believe that you will enjoy it there once you get settled. You'll have your own room as you do here, and you won't even need to work. Once we have children, we'd love for you to help."

Clara stood and walked to the window, the glass fogging with her warm breath as she watched the snowfall. "It's as cold there as it is here, isn't it?"

"Well, it can be, but not quite so windy," Robert said with an awkward smile stretching his lips. "I know this is a surprise, Clara, but it isn't like you'll be leaving much behind. Sadie and Suzanne aren't here anymore, and you work most of the time anyway. It will be an adventure." He raised his cup to Clara and Margaret.

"Yes, an adventure," Margaret repeated as she met Robert's gaze and sighed.

Clara rubbed the bridge of her nose, her head spinning. "And when are we to leave?"

Robert broke her gaze and reached for the poker for the fire, reaching in and turning a log over. "Well, that's the thing. It's an emergency, so we'll be leaving by the end of the month."

Clara frowned, turning toward Margaret. "That's less than two weeks."

Margaret's smile grew even bigger as she clapped her hands together. "Yes, isn't it exciting? I can't wait to see New York. I've never been…all the tall buildings, Central Park and all the excitement. And Clara, we can go shopping."

Clara scrunched her nose at the thought of shopping. Not only shopping with Margaret, which could be very tiring as she carried all of the bags of clothes Margaret bought. But really about shopping at all. Period. It wasn't something that she enjoyed.

Holding her hands out toward the fire, Clara sighed. Robert was right. With Sadie and Suzanne gone, she really didn't have much to leave. She was sure there were bakeries in New York, and supposed she could get a job there as well.

"Thank you for letting me know," she said. "I'm tired. If you'll excuse me..."

"Yes, yes, of course." Margaret stood and gave her a quick hug. Tucking a loose piece of Clara's red, wavy hair behind her ear, she whispered, "It will be grand fun, Clara. You'll see."

Clara tried to smile at her and her brother as she turned to walk up the stairs, her stomach twisted in knots. Halfway up, she heard Robert say, "Well, that went quite well, don't you think?"

She opened the door to her room and plopped down on the bed, falling backwards and staring at the ceiling. An adventure, they'd said. New York didn't sound much like the kind of adventure she'd be interested in, but Robert and Margaret seemed positive that they'd like it. She rolled the proposition around in her mind, remembering she'd always been more interested in traveling, but of a different kind...ones that involved animals, or trees or...well, just places that weren't full of tall buildings.

She sat bolt upright, remembering the letter she'd gotten the other day from Sadie. She opened the drawer of her nightstand, rummaging until she found it. She hadn't responded to Sadie's letter. In fact, she'd forgotten all about it, until now.

She opened the envelope, a sprig of lavender falling out that she hadn't noticed before. She brought it to her nose and inhaled deeply, reveling in the scent and imagining what it might look like where Suzanne and Sadie lived. Arizona Territory, was it?

She unfolded the letter and read it again. By the time she'd finished, her heart felt full at the faint glimmer of hope. Hope for a different life than her brother and sister-in-law wanted for her.

She took a deep breath, setting the letter down. She stood and walked to the window, pressing her hand on the cold pane of glass, ice crystals collecting in the corners.

Could she be a bride to someone she'd never met? To a wrangler, no less—not that she knew what a wrangler was, but she was pretty sure it involved something to do with horses—who needed a wife to inherit land?

Gazing at the tall, gray buildings surrounding her and the snow gathering on the ground, she made her decision. As she headed down the stairs to tell her brother and Margaret she'd be going to Arizona Territory instead of New York, she wondered if it snowed in Arizona. She shrugged her shoulders and skipped the last step, her heart fluttering with excitement at the leap of faith she would be taking. But it was *her* leap of faith.

Chapter Two

he three-day train ride had gone by quickly for Clara. She slept most of the way, exhausted by the sheer activity of helping Robert and Margaret pack for their move to New York. It had been a bittersweet week—they'd tried every day to change her mind—but she'd held steadfast. That alone had been exhausting, not to mention the wrapping of delicate china, clocks and trinkets—all the while assuring Margaret that her trip to Arizona Territory wouldn't be the end of her.

"You don't even know this person," Margaret said almost every day. Sometimes more than once a day.

Clara had held firm in her decision, explaining that Sadie and Suzanne had spoken highly of Hank Archer, and reminded Margaret that they'd all known Sadie, Suzanne and their parents their whole lives. She trusted them, and she encouraged Margaret to do the same.

By the time she'd actually gotten on the train and waved her final goodbyes to Robert, who was trying very hard to smile, and Margaret, who was dabbing her eyes with a handkerchief, she was ready to go. Exhausted, but ready. When she'd fallen asleep, it had been a sleep borne of countless waking hours and she sunk into it, rousing only for necessities and food, missing the changing scenery.

She blinked the sleep out of her eyes as the conductor came through and shouted, "Next stop, Benson, Arizona Territory. Thirty minutes to Benson."

She turned and watched him as he exited into the following car, stunned that the entire trip had gone by so quickly. She sat up straight, her muscles objecting as she stretched. Used to long hours in the bakery, she stood and stretched more, oblivious to the glances of the other passengers. Out the window, strange vegetation whizzed past—she thought maybe there were cactuses but she'd never seen one. As she straightened her hair and tucked it back under her crumpled hat, the cactuses gave way to tall trees as they crossed a bridge over a river—or at least a riverbed. Frost hung in the trees and the riverbed was dry, but as she placed her hand on the window, she smiled at the warmth it transmitted. It was nowhere near as cold as Chicago.

She'd written Sadie with her arrival date but hadn't heard back from her—one of the reasons for Margaret's near-hysterics. Her family hadn't wanted her to get on the train with no guaranteed party waiting for her. Clara's smile spread, though, as the train pulled into the station and Sadie's warm grin met her as she stood, arm in arm, with a tall, very handsome man that Clara assumed was her new husband, Tripp.

She hopped off the train nearly as soon as it came to a full stop. Dropping her valise, she rushed into Sadie's open arms, holding tightly to her friend. Sadie pulled back, clasping Clara's hands. "Oh, dear Clara. We're so happy to see you, and thrilled that you'd decided to take Hank up on his offer—well, to help him, actually."

Clara pulled her handkerchief from her sleeve and dabbed at her face, wishing she'd taken the time to look in a mirror. She looked from her friend—certainly a sight for sore eyes—to the man smiling next to her.

Sadie laughed and grabbed his arm, pulling him closer. "Clara, this is my husband, Tripp Morgan." She smiled, looking up at him proudly, her arm through his. She leaned toward Clara, her hand to the side of her mouth, and whispered, "He's a chef."

Clara laughed, her heart warmed that her friend was so happy. And clearly in love.

"I'd heard that." She held her hand out to the man with the shy smile who seemed not to be able to take his eyes off Sadie. "Nice to meet you, Mr. Morgan," she said, shaking his hand.

"Same here, Miss Martin." He gave her hand a shake, smiling. "Welcome, and we are so grateful that you decided to come."

"I told Hank how lucky he was that you were willing. It only made him pull his hat down further and stalk away," she said, hiding her laugh with her hand.

"And I can see why you said that now." Tripp tipped his hat to Clara and made his way over to the pile of bags unloaded from the train.

As he walked away, Sadie put her arm through Clara's and turned her toward the stagecoach.

"Isn't he wonderful?" She could hardly take her eyes off of Tripp, either, and Clara wondered if it would ever be that way for her, smiling at her friend's happiness.

"And wait until you meet Hank. I really think this is a truly fortunate match. For both of you."

Clara squeezed her friend's arm. "I'm a little nervous, now that I'm here. It seemed like just a—well, a good idea, but now it's feeling more real." Her breath quickened as she thought about all of the things that it meant to be a real wife. And wasn't sure at all that she even knew what those things were.

"Don't worry. We have a long ride in the stagecoach, at least two hours. We didn't want you to have to ride alone, not knowing where you were and all. And the restaurant is closed today, so we came up to fetch you."

"And I'm so glad you did," Clara said. "I really don't even know where I am." She looked around at the strange surroundings. Buildings were much taller in Chicago than here in Arizona Territory, and the roads were even different.

Sadie guided her toward the waiting coach and

Tripp handed her bags to the driver. Clara's cheeks flushed as Tripp opened the door for them, waving them in ahead of him, and sneaked a quick peck on Sadie's cheek. "Tripp, stop that, now. We're in public."

Tripp laughed as he stepped in and closed the door behind him. Clara glanced at Sadie, whose big, blue eyes were turned to Tripp. It was easy to tell that she really hadn't mind the kiss at all.

Chapter Three

"I hope you don't mind that Hank didn't come along to meet you." Sadie still had her arm through Tripp's, where it had rested the entire trip. "We thought you might like to rest—and maybe freshen up a bit."

Clara's hands flew to her hair, tucking it back into the pins it had fallen out of. "Oh, is it that bad?"

Sadie laughed, patting her friend's knee. "No, of course not. You look lovely. I just remember the long journey and how grateful I was for a hot bath, a good meal and a real bed."

She squeezed Tripp's hand as he turned and smiled at her. "Yes, and it was nice for me to have a chance to get ready. I was nervous, too."

Sadie's eyes grew wide. "Tripp Morgan, you never told me you were nervous, too."

"How could I not be? I was marrying someone

I'd never met. Why do you think I made every dish I could think of to try to impress you?" He kissed his wife's forehead and turned to Clara. "And knowing Hank, I'm pretty sure he's feeling a little unsettled, too."

Clara sighed as she watched the river flowing alongside the road. "You know, Sadie, you told me very little in the letter you wrote. All I know is that he is a wrangler—and I don't even know what that is. And that he needs a wife to inherit property."

Tripp set his hat beside him on the seat and leaned forward, smiling. "I can't say what kind of husband he'll be, but I can fill you in on Hank Archer, the way I know him."

"Hank and Tripp grew up as brothers," Sadie added as she straightened her skirts. "They are very close."

"Yes, we are. He is like a brother to me. And we rode the trail together for years and years."

"The trail?" Clara took the pins out of her hat and set it aside as well. She rubbed her sore shoulder muscles and waited for Tripp to continue.

He leaned back in his seat, taking Sadie's hand in his. "Hank's father, Beau, is a well-known and successful rancher here around Tombstone. He has the largest herd of cattle in southern Arizona Territory. Cattle need to move...to graze and be sold...and Hank and I rode the trail from here to Texas every season to get the cattle where they needed to be."

Clara's eyes flew open. "You rode from here all the way to Texas? With cows?"

Tripp cleared his throat. "Not cows, Clara. Don't let the Archer family hear you call them cows."

Sadie laughed at Clara's surprised expression, reaching over and patting her knee once more. "Don't worry. You'll learn all of this. It can be overwhelming."

"It can. I was the cook on the trail and Hank was the best wrangler we had."

"What exactly is a wrangler?" Clara asked, not remembering that in the book she'd brought.

"A wrangler is the man who handles the extra horses. We need to take three horses per hand, so there are spares. Hank is great at it. Best I've ever seen. He keeps them in line like nobody else."

Clara sighed, wondering what she'd gotten

herself into. She had only seen horses from afar, the two most recently being the only ones she'd ever touched. And while she'd felt responsible for them, wanting to help, her knowledge and experience were—to put it mildly—very limited.

Tripp eyed her, and added, "Don't worry. You won't be expected to have anything to do with the cattle or horses. That's Beau and Hank's world."

"Well, what *will* I be doing?" Clara realized she only knew how to cook and bake, really. Yes, she loved animals, but really had no experience with them. She hoped she wouldn't be expected to milk a cow. She was used to getting milk delivered every morning, in glass bottles on the front stoop of the house.

She blinked hard when Tripp said, "If you're worried about having to milk a cow, don't be. Hank's got sisters, and they each have a job. Pepper and Rosemary are the cow-milkers."

"Pepper and Rosemary?" Clara asked. "Sisters?" Her mouth went dry. She'd only had Robert, her very much older brother, and wasn't sure what to expect with so many...sisters.

Sadie nodded her head reassuringly. "Yes.

Nutmeg, Rosemary, Sage, Saffron, Tarragon and Pepper. Their mother, Katie, was a fabulous cook and taught Tripp a great deal of what he knows. She had an herb garden she tended every day, hence the girls' names. She died not long ago. So they're all in that big, rambling house, trying to find their way. But they are very sweet girls."

Tripp and Sadie exchanged glances before Tripp continued. "It's been a rough time for them—for all of us, losing Katie. I'm sure Hank will tell you all about it, but we thought it might help for you to be prepared. It's a full house."

Clara's heart tugged at the thought of a family of that size—any size, really—losing their mother. One that was obviously loved. She wondered how she could help, how she would fit in.

"You'll see tomorrow. You're the guest of honor at the ranch for lunch. You'll meet everybody then. And you can get to know Hank. I do know that they're in a hurry for you to get married. I heard there was some sort of timeline in his grandpa's will that said he had to be married within a month after his death to inherit the property. And that's soon."

Clara shook her head, her mind fuzzy as she

tried to piece things together. "I don't understand why that would be in his grandpa's will. As a requirement."

"Nobody understands it, Clara. This was Katie's father, and she's not here to shed any light on why this might have happened. It was a big surprise to everybody, including Beau and Hank. All anybody knows is that a wife is what it will take to inherit the land. And it's land that Beau feels will be very important to the ranching operations," Tripp explained.

Sadie cleared her throat. "Yes, Beau feels it's important, so it's important."

"Now, Sadie..." Tripp took her hand and squeezed it.

"I'm sorry. I just have my opinions."

Clara and Tripp both burst out laughing. "Oh, so you know that too, Tripp?" Clara said as Sadie narrowed her eyes at them both.

"Yes, I do. Seems we have much in common, Clara. Understanding Sadie is one of them."

"And admiring her, of course," Clara said with a twinkle in her eye as she looked at her friend and realized how much she'd missed her.

Clara's heart skipped a beat as she realized where she was, and what she'd done. It suddenly hit her like a cold burst of air—she was in a different part of the country, completely foreign to her, and soon to be married to a man she'd never met. She shook her head at the strangeness of it all, wondering if she'd made the right decision.

She was relieved and comforted that Sadie liked Hank and Tripp seemed nice enough, but she sensed that there was more that they weren't telling her. A wave of exhaustion washed over her and she suddenly longed for a bath—and a bed, just as Sadie had predicted. Closing her eyes and leaning her head back against the seat of the coach, her exhaustion got the best of her.

"Clara? Clara, are you all right?" Sadie said, leaning forward.

She slowly opened her eyes, rubbing them with her handkerchief. Tripp's furrowed brow and Sadie's frown shook her out of her musings.

"Oh, please don't worry. It's been a long journey, and I'm very tired. I wanted this—I do want this—and I'm very anxious to meet Hank. All of them, actually.

Her smile felt weak, but it was there. She hoped that after she'd gotten some rest, she might feel a little more like smiling. Right now, though, all she wanted was sleep. Tripp and Sadie fell silent as Clara's head fell to the side, her mind free of worry—for now.

Chapter Four

Clara's eyes fluttered open and for a moment, she wasn't sure where she was. The terrain out the window had changed again, and she saw what she thought were tall cactuses, based on the pictures she'd seen. She reached into her valise and pulled out a worn book, rubbing her hand over the soft leather that covered it. She opened it to a page with pictures of cactus and tried to match the pictures to what she saw out the window.

Tripp and Sadie dozed in the seat across from her, Sadie's head resting on Tripp's shoulder, and Clara smiled. She breathed a sigh of relief at the sight of them so comfortable together, her heart swelling at the thought that she might have something like that too, one day.

She set the book on her lap and breathed in the cool, fresh air. It was the beginning of spring, and the late winter snowstorm recently before she'd left Chicago made her appreciate the warmth here even more. Out the window, she saw a beautiful stand of trees that were definitely not cactuses. Tall, leafy and very green, she opened her book and flipped through to see if she could find something similar, even a drawing. Not finding anything, she turned to look again, shielding her eyes against the bright rays of the sun.

At the base of the trees she could see the figure of a man—too far away to see any features, but she could make out a cowboy hat. The man stood, looking at something that was over the horizon, too far away for her to see. He leaned against a tree and put his hand to his mouth. She heard a faint whistle, and couldn't look away.

The scene was so foreign to her, and she gasped as she saw a beautiful, white horse slowly walk up to him. It stopped a few feet away, and he held out his hand to it.

She gasped when the horse moved the remaining distance toward him, nuzzling his chest as he stroked its nose. Mesmerized, she watched him grab its reins and leap on its back, taking off in the opposite direction at full speed after a brief wave in her direction, she assumed to the driver of the stagecoach.

She was ripped from her thoughts by the stagecoach driver's yell of, "Coming into Tombstone, folks. Fifteen minutes." Clara laughed as both Tripp and Sadie sat bolt upright, clearly startled by the shout. Sadie rubbed her eyes then glanced out the window. "Yep, we're here. And there's Suzanne to pick us up."

Clara spied Suzanne, each hand clasping that of a beautiful little girl who looked exactly like each other. "Oh, my. It's going to be just the same as growing up with you two, isn't it?"

Tripp leaned forward and looked out the window. "Ah, yes. That takes some getting used to. First these twins, Sadie and Suzanne, and then another two with Lucy and Lily."

"They are adorable," Clara said as she leaned out the window, waving at Suzanne.

"Maybe it's something in the water around here. Hank has two sisters that are twins, too. Wonder if it'll be like that with us." Tripp kissed the back of Sadie's hand.

Sadie's smile wasn't quite as big as it usually was as her face turned pink and she patted Tripp's knee. "Let's not rush into anything there, Mr.

Morgan."

Tripp raised an eyebrow and winked at Clara. "I think she's a little nervous."

"I am no such thing," Sadie said, pulling her hand away from Tripp's and turning toward the window.

As the coach slowed to a stop, Tripp hopped out, holding out his hand as each of the girls stepped down.

Clara spotted Suzanne again and rushed to her, grasping her friend in a firm hug. Her smile widened as she bent down, eye level to the two little girls with long, blonde braids hanging down their backs. "And who have we here? And how do I tell you apart?" Clara said, looking from one twin to the other."

"Oh, don't mind them. They're usually very—"

"Mama says there is no way to tell us apart, but we know who we are. I'm Lucy, and this is my sister Lily," said one of the twins, pointing at herself and then thrusting her thumb at her sister.

Clara put her hand to her mouth to stifle a giggle. She hadn't had much experience with children, but enjoyed being around them when she'd had the opportunity. She looked again for a moment from Lucy to Lily. "Hmm. I bet I can tell you apart. I will practice."

Both the girls giggled. "We're glad to meet you," Lucy said, making a small curtsy.

Clara laughed and took off her gloves, shaking their hands and curtsying herself. "So glad to make your acquaintance, Lucy and Lily."

She stood and blinked hard as Suzanne stared at her, mouth agape. "I was going to say shy. I've never seen them greet anyone like that right away."

"Oh, really? I can't imagine that. They're so friendly," she said and looked down as two little hands grabbed hers. She smiled at Suzanne and shrugged.

"Well, that's a first," Sadie said from behind her. "Took me a lot longer, but you've always had that way about you." She smiled, looping her arm through Suzanne's. "Come on, this way. Tripp's got your bags and will bring around the buggy."

Clara followed her friends as she squeezed the girls' hands and felt a squeeze back. She breathed deeply, taking in her surroundings. Robert was her only sibling, and she'd grown up with Sadie and Suzanne. They were as close as sisters to her. Being with them now warmed her heart as much as it had back in Chicago, and gratitude washed over her as she walked behind them, Lucy and Lily in tow.

They'd both wanted to sit next to her in the buggy and talked the entire ride home. Suzanne had turned back once or twice, shaking her head at the girls and shrugging her shoulders. She smiled at Clara, and once said, "Let me know if you need some relief."

Clara smiled and paid very close attention to the things the girls were pointing out—the mercantile, Tripp and Sadie's restaurant, the church, the theater. "This is much bigger than I'd imagined it to be," Clara said as they pulled up in front of a big, white house with two stories and a big porch wrapped around three sides.

"It's even so big you can get lost," Lucy said.

"Only if you don't know where you're going." Lily crossed her arms over her chest. "She gets lost a lot."

"Do not," Lucy said, folding her arms over her

chest as well.

"Come on, chatterboxes. Let's give Clara a little break," Suzanne said as she reached up into the buggy to lift the girls down, one at a time. "Run into the house and see Daddy."

Turning to Clara, she said, "Whew. They really were giving you quite the tour, weren't they?"

"I was grateful for it. I really haven't spent any time out of Chicago, so this is all new to me. It's a lovely little town. Well, a big town. Bigger than I'd expected."

Tripp reached up to help Sadie out of the buggy, then Clara. "It's grown quite a bit since that silver vein was found. Grew fast. Almost too fast. We're not really in Tombstone proper, but it's the biggest place close by," he said as he tied the leather reins to the post in front of the house.

"And who lives here?" Clara looked up at the big house and smiled. She'd never had her own house, and now, in her mid-twenties like Sadie and Suzanne, was anxious to have one of her own. She'd grow flowers out front in the spring, and have herbs in the garden to cook with. Her heart fluttered at the thought of a home of her own.

"This is Suzanne's house," Sadie said, looping her arm through Clara's and pulling her toward the stairs to the porch. "She has more bedrooms here than we do. Tripp's adding on to our house for..well.."

"You're blushing, my friend. Do you mean for children?" Clara laughed and squeezed her friend's hand. Clara remembered how strong and sure Sadie had always been—but she'd never seen her around a man. Maybe this was different. She'd rarely seen her out of the bakery back home after Suzanne left for Arizona Territory and Sadie took over the business when their parents died. She sighed, grateful that her friend had found a good man, and a good life.

Sadie turned to look at Tripp, who was smiling widely at her and seemed almost ready to laugh outright. "This woman, I tell you. Yes, we're adding rooms for children. Now, if you'll excuse me, I'm going to start on supper while you ladies get settled." He turned to Clara and tipped his hat before holding the door open for the ladies. "I'll bring Clara's bags up and set them in the hall."

"Goodness, he cooks at home, too?" Clara said, her eyebrows raised.

Suzanne laughed as she turned at the top of the stairs and ushered Clara into a beautiful bedroom that had obviously had Suzanne's decorating touch. The calm colors of green, purple and white soothed her senses and she sat on the bed, a rush of exhaustion coming back as the excitement subsided.

"He cooks when I let him, and he's fairly good at it. Mostly, he's my sous chef at home, but tonight he's on his own. Wanted to make something special." Sadie winked at Suzanne and smiled. "You never know with him, though, so I'd better go supervise. I'll see you at supper after you rest for a bit," she said with a hug for Clara before she left and closed the door behind her.

"She sure looks happy." Clara reached up and took the pins out of her hat and set them on the vanity, resting her hat on a hook by the door.

Suzanne smoothed out the bedspread and brought some towels out of a drawer. "She sure is. It was touch and go there for a while, but they've seemed to find a happy rhythm. The restaurant is wonderful, and I'm sure you'll be going there soon. For tonight, though, you'll be getting a Tripp and Sadie original."

"Oh, goodness. I hope they're not going to much trouble on my account."

"You know as well as I do, Clara Martin, that Sadie's in hog heaven cooking for you. And her husband is, too. Trust me. Oh, and Hank will be coming for supper, too. I'll bring up water for a bath, and you just relax best you can. Been a long journey, I'm sure."

"I...I...he is?" Clara's face flushed and she found herself wringing her hands. She'd known this time was coming but now that it was imminent, the butterflies in her belly had re-awakened.

Suzanne sat down on the bed beside Clara, smoothing a stray lock of her red, wavy hair back. "I imagine you're a bit nervous. I sure would be. But, Clara, you know you are like a sister to us. Hank is a very good friend—like a brother—of Tripp's. Sadie's gotten to know him even better than I have, and she really believes that there's something about you two that is special. I trust her, and for now, can you? You don't have to go through with this if you don't want to."

Clara looked down at her hands and smoothed her skirts. She stood and reached into her valise, pulling out the book about the Wild West frontier and handing it to Suzanne. "I left because I wanted a change and a family, Suzanne, and I aim to have one. I'm not afraid, just a little anxious."

"I would be surprised if you *weren't* nervous," Suzanne said. She flipped through the pages of the picture book quickly. "Can I borrow this while you're napping? I'd like to show the girls."

"Thank you. I'll be back with water for your bath. Make yourself comfortable." Suzanne tucked the book under her arms and opened the door.

"Thank you, Suzanne. For everything." Clara reached to the vase of lavender on the vanity and picked it up, holding it under her nose as she breathed deeply.

Suzanne poked her head back in the door as she drew it closed. "You're welcome for everything. I am so happy you're here." She nodded her head, her smile ear to ear.

Chapter Five

Clara had just finished braiding her hair as the knock came at the door. It had taken much longer than usual, her fingers fumbling as she thought of Hank Archer, her future—she could barely allow herself to even think the word. But it was husband. And she'd better get used to it. She'd soon be Clara Archer, a thought that made the butterflies explode in a full-fledged swarm.

The door opened and one of the twins' head poked in. "Who am I?" she said, her little face defying Clara to answer correctly. Clara had taken the time during the buggy ride to notice enough about the girls to tell them apart. The differences were very subtle, but she had an idea and welcomed the distraction from the butterflies to try out her theory.

"Hmm. Can you step in closer so I can see better?" Clara sat down on the bed and patted next to her. The twin threw the door open and walked forward, sitting next to Clara as she looked toward the door.

"Come in so Clara can see you," she said to her sister, who had barely poked her eyes around the side of the door.

"Ah, I can tell you right now. You are Lucy." She hugged the little girl next to her. Pointing to the door, she said, "And you are Lily."

The girls dissolved into giggles so infectious that Clara couldn't help but laugh, too.

"How did you know? Nobody *ever* knows," Lucy said as she settled back down.

"I have my ways, and it's a secret." Clara stood and took one last glance in the mirror. The butterflies started again, and she tugged at the sleeves of her dress that was still a bit wrinkled although she'd laid it out before she'd bathed and napped.

Lily reached out and picked up the drop pearl earrings Clara had debated wearing, wondering if they were too much for the occasion. As the tiny hand held the earrings out to her, she took them in her palm, her green eyes searching Lily's face.

"You need to wear these," Lily said.

"Yes, you look beautiful," Lucy said, dancing around the bedroom.

Clara turned again to the mirror, fastening the earrings on her ears, blinking back tears. How could Lily, who she knew now to be the more shy, sensitive twin, have known that these were the earrings her mother left her before she'd moved away, telling her in the note if she ever needed courage to wear these, and her mother would be with her in spirit.

She bent down and kissed Lily on the cheek. "Thank you, Lily. I needed that."

Both girls' eyes grew wide at the knock at the door downstairs. They ran out the door and peeked through the stairway railings to the foyer, turned and ran back into the room.

"Hurry, Clara, hurry. Hank's here," Lucy said, grabbing her hand and pulling her toward the door. Lucy took her other hand and looked up to Clara, smiling and squeezing her hand.

Clara took a deep breath, stood tall and walked toward her fate.

CHAPTER SIX

Clara was careful not to trip on her way down the stairs as the twins pulled and tugged. She'd been watching her feet to make sure that her introduction to her future husband did not involve a tumble down the stairs and her sprawled on the floor, so when she reached the bottom and the girls let go of her hands and ran to the kitchen, it was her first opportunity to look up. When she did, it was all she could do to suppress a gasp as she looked up into the kindest face she'd ever seen, with sparkling blue eyes and dark hair brushed back away from his face. He held his hat over his heart, his face flushed but his eyes twinkling. She was unable to find her voice as her head tilted to the side and she studied the laugh lines around his eyes, sure that he'd spent quite a bit of time outside in the elements to have them, but relieved they were laugh lines rather than frown lines.

"Hank Archer, this is Clara Martin. Clara,

Hank. And while I'm at it, this is my husband James." Suzanne pulled a man forward, smiling up at him. He was quite tall, and as Clara turned to him, he held out his hand with a smile as broad as Suzanne's.

"Very nice to meet you, James," Clara said, welcoming the brief break she'd gotten before she had to actually speak to Hank. She knew she couldn't possibly have met him before, but there seemed to be something very familiar about him. She wasn't quite sure what, so she just held out her hand and smiled. "And to meet you, too, Hank."

He quickly wiped his hand on his pants before extending it to her, which she thought must be a habit from being outside so much as right now, he was very clean and dressed in a nice jacket with some sort of string tie, clasped together with a turquoise stone set in silver and shining in the light of the foyer. He even smelled nice—masculine, but nice.

He tipped his head slightly as he shook her hand, his eyes cast at the floor. When he looked up again, the twinkle remained and his smile returned as they both looked to Suzanne.

"Oh, yes, right. Please come this way. Tripp and

Sadie have dinner ready for us," she said, looping her arms through both Clara and Hank's. She pulled them forward as Hank reached behind him and tossed his hat to James, who caught it with a smile and hung it on the hat rack by the door. "You're going to love this."

Clara smiled as she reached the table. Taking in the roast chicken, mashed potatoes and gravy, and spying the apple pie on the sideboard, she clapped her hands, looking to her dear friend, Sadie, as warmth spread across her chest. "All my favorites," she said, sighing. "Thank you."

Sadie and Tripp exchanged smiles, and Sadie said, "We wanted to make you feel welcome, and at home. It is a long journey, and if I remember correctly, very nerve-wracking."

She squeezed Tripp's hand as she spread her other across the table. "Sit down, everybody. It's here for us to enjoy."

Clara jumped at the feel of Hank's hand on her elbow as he gently guided her to a place setting and pulled out her chair for her, scooting her forward as she sat. She'd never been courted before—too busy working and no time for it—and she wondered if this was part of it.

She shook her head, as he wouldn't have to court her. They were just going to get married for the property, so she pushed any thoughts of a relationship out of her mind.

Sadie and Suzanne filled her in about the Occidental and how it had come to be such a success, with only occasional good-natured objections of fact from Tripp.

"Actually, it's Hank and his father we should thank," Sadie said, smiling at Hank as she handed him a piece of apple pie. "If you and your father hadn't asked for Tripp's trail cooking, who knows where we'd be."

Hank cleared his throat. He hadn't spoken much during the meal so far, and Clara was anxious to hear him speak. To get to know him better, even though it really didn't matter.

"It was really just something we thought Tripp might actually like to do if he thought about it. And also something we'd been sorely deprived of when he was away in New York." He popped the last bite of one of Sadie's biscuits in his mouth and picked up his fork to start in on the pie.

Tripp nodded his head briefly at Hank. "Thank

you for the compliment, and I suppose all's well that ends well."

Sadie stood up and began to clear dishes off the table. "Would anyone like coffee?"

A unanimous "yes" sent her toward the kitchen.

Tripp leaned back in his chair. "So, Hank, any more news about the property? We were able to fill Clara in a little bit on the coach ride down, but not too much."

"Well, how much did you get to say?" Hank set his napkin down on his plate, scooting back a bit with his eyebrows raised at Tripp.

"I can answer that," said Clara, dabbing her mouth with her napkin. "I know that you inherited property from your grandfather. I know that you need a wife to claim the inheritance. And I know that there's a timeline in the will."

Hank rubbed the back of his neck. "Then it sounds like you know about as much as I do, Miss."

"I'm a bit confused, though," Clara said, looking from Hank to Tripp. "Is the property particularly valuable? Especially large? I would think that taking a wife whom you don't know is a fairly extreme measure for a piece of property."

Tripp turned from Hank to Clara. "It's a bit of a long story, but the property is adjacent to Hank's father's ranch. If Hank wasn't in a position to inherit the property on his grandfather's death, the property was slated to go to someone else. Apparently, Mr. Archer feels it's important to keep it in the family. Probably because it's prime grazing land."

"That's right," Hank added. "That's all we can think of as to why Pa is so adamant about this happening. I mean, it's a nice chunk of land, but I'm not even sure how my mother's father ended up with it in the first place. And Pa's not been too willing to talk about it."

"That's rather curious." Clara twisted her napkin on her lap as she waited for more of the story.

"Maybe we'll find out more about it tomorrow," Hank said, shrugging his shoulders.

"Tomorrow?" Clara questioned Suzanne.

"Yes, Mr. Archer has a big fiesta planned in honor of your arrival, Clara. It's at the Archer Ranch, which is beautiful. You'll love it."

Clara felt the butterflies return as the reality of the situation set in. Now she'd meet his family. Soon enough, *she* would be family. Or at least formally.

"Is that all right with you, Miss? We'd be mighty pleased to have all of you come out. You must be wondering what you've gotten yourself into."

Clara's heart pounded in her chest as she looked at Hank, his hopefulness impossible to ignore.

"Of course, I'd be happy to come. I look forward to meeting my future family, as well as seeing the ranch.

Hank's smile spread even wider as he breathed a sigh that Clara thought sounded like relief. "Thank you, Miss. Tripp, are you willing to bring everyone out, or should I come to fetch people?"

"No, James and I can handle it, Hank, but thanks. If everything's the same as it used to be, you'll be needed for preparations."

Hank's face clouded as he stood and reached for his hat. "Nothing's changed there, Tripp," he said, his voice low. He turned to Sadie. "Thank you for the wonderful supper, Morgan family. I'll be taking my leave as I imagine Miss Martin could use some more rest."

Lucy and Lily jumped out of their seats and each hugged one of Hank's knees. "Can we ride tomorrow, Uncle Hank? Can we?" Lucy tugged at his sleeve while Lily stood silent, her blue eyes not leaving his face.

Hank squatted and gave both of the girls a hug. "We'll see, little ladies. Not sure what's on the agenda for tomorrow, but if I can saddle up for you, I sure will."

The girls squealed as they ran upstairs, their mother right behind them. "Night, Hank. We'll see you tomorrow," Suzanne said as she disappeared after the twins.

Clara laughed as she stood and turned toward Hank. "They're quite a handful."

Hank and Tripp exchanged looks. "You think *they* are a handful. Wait until you meet my six sisters," Hank said with a shake of his head.

"Oh, they're all right," Tripp said. "If a little…busy." He clapped Hank on the back as they walked toward the door.

Hank shook hands with James and Tripp, and nodded his head at Sadie and Clara before he turned toward the door. "Busy. Is that what you call it? We'll see how tomorrow goes. Good night, and thank you again for the fine supper."

As Hank closed the door behind him, Clara spun toward Sadie. "Six? Really six sisters?"

Sadie picked up more dishes and said over her shoulder on the way to the kitchen, "Yes, six. But they're a lot of fun. The twins love them."

Clara sat back down, and the butterflies returned. Six sisters? And his father a widower? Her last thought before she headed into the kitchen to help with the dishes was to wonder who looked after all of them. She wasn't sure if she was prepared for it to be her.

Clara lifted the twins into the buggy as she waited for the others to come. She'd woken early, before sunrise, and hadn't been able to go back to sleep. She'd brushed her hair at least a thousand times before braiding it, undoing it and braiding it again until she heard people downstairs. Her nerves wouldn't calm down enough for her to do anything else.

As she lifted her skirts and pulled herself up into the buggy, she hoped that her new family would like her. And that she'd like them. She breathed deeply, inhaling the scent of sage as they passed different types of trees and plants. "Suzanne, did you show the twins the picture in the book I brought?"

"Oh, I did. Wasn't that fun, girls? The book we looked at before bedtime last night."

"Yes," Lucy said as Lily nodded. "I liked the pictures of the cowboys on horses."

Tripp laughed. "I think some of those might be wranglers. Like Uncle Hank."

"What's a wrangler, mama?" Lucy said, turning to her mother.

"What exactly is a wrangler, Tripp? You'd likely be the best to explain."

They all turned to Tripp and even Sadie waited for his response. "Well, what is it? You used to be one, didn't you?"

As James guided the horses down the road to the ranch, he said, "He did, but the wrangler life isn't for everybody. It can be a pretty rough life."

Tripp sighed and took Sadie's hand. "Yes, it is a tough life. Being out on the trail for weeks at a time can take a real toll. It's fun for a while, but sleeping on the ground and even eating my cooking—"

"That would have made it all okay, wouldn't it," Sadie teased, smiling up at her husband.

"I'd like to think so, but no. It's a rough life. It's really better for the younger men with no family. In fact, the last few times I've talked to Hank, he's made noise about being close to done, himself. Wanting to stay put." Tripp looked ahead at the big ranch house that was coming closer as he spoke, a frown appearing. "But that remains to be seen. Beau seems to want him out there still, and Beau usually gets what he wants."

Clara's breath hitched as she listened. She hadn't really known what a wrangler was, but now that she'd heard, would Hank be gone most of the time?

The group fell quiet as they approached the ranch, the silence broken by the squeals of the girls as their buggy passed a barn that seemed huge to

Clara. Peering in as they passed, she counted at least ten horse stalls lining the inside, five on each side. Each had horses peering out, their whinnies reminding her of the cold horses she'd tried to help in Chicago.

"I've just recently gotten to know horses, and I love them," she said as they passed by.

"We do, too!" Lucy cried. "I hope we get to ride today."

Suzanne smoothed her daughter's hair. "Now, remember, Uncle Hank wasn't sure if we were going to be able to do that today. The party is for Clara, so we'll have to be patient. If not today, maybe we can come a different day."

Lucy's bottom lip stuck out so far Clara laughed that it might stay that way, as her mother had always told her it would. The thought of her mother jolted her back to the matter at hand, and as she looked up at the house of her future family, she felt a tug at her heart, wishing her mother were here with her now. She reached up to her ears, reassuring herself that the earrings her mother had given her were there. She'd need all the courage she could get today. And probably tomorrow, too.

Although Clara had expected mostly cactuses and sand, she looked up at full trees as they passed through two long lines of them on each side of the entrance road to the main house. After they'd passed the barn, before they'd reached what she assumed to be the main house, they passed a smaller house, one story, and made from something different than the wood she was used to. The white walls shimmered in the spring sun and she admired the bright blue of the windowsills. It was certainly different than anything she'd ever seen.

Outside of the small house was what looked like an herb garden, but it was apparent that it hadn't been tended to in quite some time. Its bushes had fallen over, and weeds had pierced their way through most of the small groups of plants, most of which Clara recognized from her sister-in-law's greenhouse she'd had, full of herbs that they'd used for cooking.

Curious about the state of the garden, she turned to Suzanne who quietly shook her head and nodded toward Tripp. Clara frowned as she saw him look away toward the house, his somber expression discouraging questions of any kind.

James slowed the buggy as they drew closer to the house, and Clara's nerves jangled as Hank walked down the steps of the porch, tipping his hat to them before he took the reins from James. He held the buggy while they got out, their skirts flouncing as they hit the ground.

Just as everyone had gotten out of the buggy, they all turned at the sound of one of the horses neighing and its bridle clanking as it reared its head. The buggy pulled forward as it did, and James and Suzanne pulled the twins back further toward the house.

Clara watched as Hank pulled the reins in tighter and heard him speak to the horse under his breath, all the while stroking its nose. The horse's ears turned toward him as it stomped once and quieted, nuzzling Hanks hand.

Hank smiled, keeping eye contact with the horse as he gave him a final pat and whispered something again. He handed the reins to a young man and said, "Take them around to the barn with the others. Thanks, Ben."

He watched the horses round the corner before he turned toward the group. His eyebrows rose as he took in the group, mouths agape as they'd watched the scene.

"What?" he said, holding his arms open wide.

"How do you do that, Hank? Even out on the trail, you were the only one who could calm these horses, even in the wildest of times," Tripp said, shaking his head.

"Nah," Hank said, pulling his hat further down his forehead. "Anybody can do it."

Tripp sighed as he turned toward the house, holding his arm out to Sadie.

Hank held his arm out to Clara, and she smiled and took it with her own. She frowned at Sadie when she winked at her, and turned her attention back to Hank and the house. As they reached the porch, Hank stopped and she thought she heard him say under his breath, "Uh-oh."

She turned her gaze to the direction he was looking, and her eyes flew open wide as a line of girls rushed past and into the door, pigtails flying. The shortest one, about sixteen years old, Clara guessed, stopped in front of the twins. She bent over, her hands on her knees as she tried to catch her breath. "Want to come with us? We're late getting ready and Papa's mad, but you can come help, if you want. There's somebody special coming and we have to look like girls."

Suzanne looked down at the pleading eyes of Lucy and Lily. "Promise me you'll mind Pepper," she said to the girls' vigorous nods. She placed their hands in the girl's and shook her head. "Be good, now. And Pepper, this is Clara, the special guest."

Pepper stood slowly, her face panicked as she stared, open-mouthed, at the twins. She sighed, and turned around, smiling at her brother and Clara. "It's nice to meet you. I'm not supposed to see you yet, though, until I get ready. Please don't tell anyone, and I'll meet you again in a little bit."

She turned to Hank, her puppy-eyed face having its intended results.

"Scoot. Get along. Pa's not up here yet, anyway."

Pepper jumped up and down, gathered the twins' hands in her own and disappeared in the house.

"So that's how it goes when I'm not looking, eh?" a voice boomed behind Clara, down at the bottom of the stairs.

Clara felt Hank's arm stiffen in hers. They all turned toward the voice, which apparently belonged to a tall, handsome man with dark hair, graying around the temples. "Hello, Mr. Archer," Suzanne said as she put her arm through James's and squeezed.

"Yes, hello," Tripp said as he took Sadie's hand in his.

Clara wasn't exactly sure what to say, so she waited for Hank.

"Hi, Pa. The girls were on their way to get dressed, like you asked, and Pepper stopped to take Lucy and Lily with them."

"Yes, I saw that. They were to have been dressed and ready an hour ago." The man shook his head as he climbed the steps. It seemed to Clara that everyone on the porch had all agreed to hold their breath at the same time. And she felt them all exhale together as Mr. Archer said, "And this must be your future bride, Clara," extending his hand to her with a tip of his hat and a wide smile.

"Pa, meet Clara Martin. Clara, my father, Beau Archer."

He bowed slightly to Clara as he shook her hand. "Delighted to meet you, young lady. We've been anxiously expecting you."

"Thank you, Mr. Archer. I have—"

"Please, call me Beau. And let's go inside. We should be starting soon."

Both Clara and Hank stared at his back as he turned and entered the house, his boots loud on the porch as he strode ahead of them.

Tripp followed with Sadie on his arm. He clapped Hank on his shoulder as he passed. "It'll be all right. Let's just go on in," he said, giving him a reassuring smile.

Hank breathed in heavily and let it out hard. He turned to smile at Clara and patted her hand that was on his arm.

"His bark is worse than his bite. I promise," he said as he ushered her into the home of what would be her new family.

Chapter Seven

After the lunch Beau had planned, Clara had gotten a brief tour of the unusual house and had learned that it was made of something called adobe, a clay mixture dried and used as blocks.

"This is what many people who are native to this climate use to build their homes, and Pa wanted to try it," Hank explained as they walked past the thick, solid walls. "Makes it cooler in summer and warmer in winter, keeping out most of the cold drafts and heat."

He'd been giving a running commentary—she wasn't sure if it was due to nerves—since they'd begun their tour, telling her about the art, the furniture and where it had come from.

When they got to the kitchen, though, he walked straight through without a word. Clara glanced back at the glimmering pots and pans hanging from the ceiling and the stove that seemed to be big enough to feed a crowd of this size. He hadn't seemed to want to stop there, so she held her tongue and finished the tour.

As they sat in the living room, she glanced out the windows to the back of the house. The vivid blue window frames of the smaller house she'd seen earlier caught her eye and she craned her neck, trying to see the garden from this vantage point.

She felt a tap on her elbow and turned quickly, almost bumping into the cups Hank held in his hands.

"Oh, I'm sorry," she said with a laugh. "I wasn't paying attention." She accepted the cup he offered and took a sip, the tart taste of lemonade welcome on her tongue. The lunch they'd eaten had some spices in it that Clara hadn't recognized. She'd like it very much, but it had left a slow burn in her mouth that she was unaccustomed to.

Hank smiled and looked past her to where she'd had her gaze. "Oh," he said, glancing down at his cup of lemonade.

Clara frowned as his face clouded and he sighed.

"Oh?" she repeated, not entirely sure what he'd

meant. It was clear to her that he wasn't very enthusiastic about talking about what was bothering him, either here or in the kitchen, but if she was to marry this man, there could be no secrets, no matter what kind of relationship it was. A marriage was a marriage, and right was right.

He took Clara's lemonade from her hand and set both his cup and hers on the table by the settee. Opening the door to the patio, he pulled her outside and shut it behind them. "Is that what you were curious about?" he said, pointing to the little white house with the blue shutters.

She turned to see what he was pointing at, nodding slowly. "Yes, it is. It has a garden that could use some tending, and—"

"Clara, I know this might be difficult to understand, but there are some things we just don't talk about around here."

Her heart leapt to her throat as she walked to the edge of the lovely brick patio, staring in the direction of the little house. She was in new territory—literally—and while she was used to speaking her mind, she had gotten a sense that this was a family that didn't talk much to each other. She'd felt the weight of it as soon as she'd entered the property, and even more strongly when she'd entered the house.

People were kind enough, but very ill at ease. Tripp's words about Katie, Hank and the girls' mother and Beau's wife, rang in her ears. She'd passed away, and not that long ago. She wondered if it was sorrow that still held them all in its grip.

She put her hands behind her and leaned against the wall as he slowly paced back and forth on the patio. The pillar holding up the patio roof squeaked as he leaned against it, looking over toward the small house.

"We don't know each other all that well yet, Hank, but I'm not normally one to keep secrets—or tiptoe around things. I hope that won't be a problem. I know some things are private, but if I'm going to be part of this family, even in name only, and be expected to live here, I need to be let in."

Hank looked down at his feet, scuffing his boots on the floor. "Clara, I—"

"Pa says to come back in the house, Hank. It's time," Pepper said as she poked her head out the door.

He stood, his arms folded over his chest. "Time

for what?"

"Just come on," she said as she swung the door open wider and ran back into the house.

Hank held his arm out for Clara and said, "Can we talk later, Clara? This is all new to me, and I…"

She stopped, meeting his gaze as she turned to him. "Of course. And thank you for being willing." She started to raise her hand to his cheek and her heart tugged as she drew her hand back, realizing that she barely knew this man. Grateful that he'd agreed to talk to her later, she followed him inside the house.

"There you two are," Beau said as he opened his arms wide and gestured for them to sit on the settee in front of the fireplace. "Come warm up by the fire. It's cold out there."

Clara hadn't noticed the cold. It was certainly nothing like the snow in Chicago, but she sat down by the fire anyway and Hank sat beside her.

"It's time you met the rest of the family, Clara," Beau said and he frowned in Hank's direction as she heard him groan. "Your sisters are very happy for you, as am I, and they prepared something for you. Girls?"

Clara laughed with delight as six girls, stair-stepped in height but for the middle two who were clearly twins, walked out from the dining room in matching pinafores. The tallest one spoke first as she smiled at her brother and Clara.

The girls stood to her right and they introduced themselves in succession, each giving a small curtsy afterward.

"I'm Nutmeg, but people call me Meg. Pleased to meet you."

"I'm Rosemary. Pleased to meet you."

"I'm Sage and this is Saffron," said one of the twins while her sister smiled and remained silent.

"I'm Tara, but really Tarragon," the next said, blushing. "Very pleased to meet you."

Clara stood and went down the line, shaking each girl's hand as she passed by. She walked slowly, looking each girl in the eye to very different reactions from each of them. Rosemary smiled and nodded. Tara lowered her eyes and immediately looked to the floor. Pepper shook her hand vigorously and laughed. When she got to Meg, the eldest, she met a very guarded young lady, who smiled with obvious effort and did not blink.

"It's nice to meet you all, as well," Clara said as she sat back down beside Hank.

Meg cleared her throat and looked at her father. He nodded and all the rest of the girls looked to their big sister.

Clara's hand flew to her chest as Meg hummed a single note and closed her eyes. With the voices of what Clara thought must be angels, Hank's sisters sang one of her favorite hymns, the harmonies of the six sisters blending in a way which Clara had never before heard, not even in church on a Sunday. Enraptured, she held her breath as they finished, breaking into applause along with all the others in the room as they finished and took a bow.

She turned to Hank, and his wide smile and loving gaze warmed her heart. She looked then at Beau, chest full as he watched his daughters with soft eyes.

"Thank you, girls," she said, jumping to her feet as the applause continued. She was met with shy grins from each girl as they hugged both their father and Hank. A pang of sadness stabbed Clara's heart, the same one she'd noticed when she'd first arrived.

A knock on the door broke the spell, and Hank shook his head quickly before opening it.

"Hello, Pastor Williams," Hank said as he shook the offered hand. "I didn't know you were coming today. What—"

Beau strode forward, shaking the man's hand and pulling him inside, ignoring the confused look on his face. "Come in, come in, Pastor. Thank you for coming."

"I'd like to introduce my...um...Clara Martin." His ears turned pink and he looked to Tripp, who was standing in the corner, watching.

The gathering had been very small, just Suzanne, Sadie and their families and the Archer family, so Clara's eyebrows rose at the sight of a new guest and the new awkwardness in the room, but she smiled as she turned to the pastor.

He shook her hand, saying, "It is very nice to meet you on such an auspicious occasion."

Hank shrugged his shoulders. "It's just lunch, but you're welcome to join us, and I'm glad you got to meet Clara before the wedding."

"Yes, well, barely," he said, laughing as he turned to Beau.

"Papa, can we start?" Pepper said, tugging at her father's sleeve.

"Start what?" Hank asked, turning to his father.

"The wedding!" Pepper cried. She grabbed the pastor's arm and pulled him forward, his face frozen as he looked from Hank to Beau.

"The what?" Hank said as he stood and took several steps toward his father.

Beau held his hands up and shook his head.

"Now, Hank, you know that the will has a timeline attached. I figured since we were in a hurry, and your intended has had the opportunity to meet the family, we'd just get on with it."

Clara watched, wide-eyed, as Hank's hands clenched into fists and unclenched again. She searched for Suzanne and Sadie, finding them as wide-eyed as she knew herself to be.

"Pa, this wasn't how I wanted this to be. Clara just arrived yesterday, and she's been gracious enough to consider my offer. I wanted to—"

Beau clapped his son on the back. "Son, son, son. There's plenty of time for that stuff later. It's getting colder, and that property will be very handy for you to use to get the cattle and the hands ready to head out on the trail next week."

"Next week?" Hank's hands had clenched permanently now and Clara stood slowly, Hank's sisters all moving behind the settee.

Beau and Hank stared at one another, neither breaking their gaze as Tripp stepped between them. Clara remembered that Suzanne had mentioned that Tripp grew up with Beau and Hank, and guessed that made him family, as well.

"Gentleman, I think you're forgetting something here." He stood between them and gestured to Clara. "It would make sense to me if the lady who'd just come all the way from Chicago had a say in when her nuptials would be…or even *if* they would be after this display."

All eyes turned to Clara, and her face flushed. She looked desperately toward Suzanne and Sadie, willing them to give her some advice and tell her what to do. Taking a deep breath and glancing out the window, she spotted the small, white house and remembered Hank's promise that they'd talk. Later. But later might be too late, and she needed to know what she was getting herself into before it was something she could not undo.

Her brother and sister-in-law's final words to her rushed into her head. "Clara, you've been taking care of yourself for a long time. Quite well, I might add, and I beg you to remember that you should do nothing that you don't feel is right for you." And her brother had pressed enough money into her hand for a train ticket to New York. "We will always be there for you."

Her head spun as all of this happened so quickly. When she heard Sadie say her name, she blinked and realized that it wasn't the first time she'd said it.

Feeling the heat of all eyes still on her, she turned to Hank and said, "I'm sorry, Hank. I can't do this so soon. I'm just not ready."

They'd gathered their things quickly and ridden home in silence after the scene between Hank and Beau—and Clara, too, she supposed. Clara's heart tugged as she thought of the look on Hank's sisters' faces when she'd said she wasn't ready to be married. And why wasn't she? She'd known that this was the reason she'd come.

Tripp and James had excused themselves to

the parlor when they arrived back home, but not before adding their opinions.

"That was pretty bold, even for Beau," Tripp had said, shaking his head. "That tops just about everything else I've seen."

James nodded as they headed out of the kitchen. "I don't know him as well as Tripp does, but that was unusually bold for the man I know."

Clara sat down on the chair next to her. "Does he do these things frequently? Totally disregard others' opinions or feelings?"

Tripp sighed. "Beau is a very successful rancher, and has been since the beginning. He's used to getting his way—and also used to getting things done. He and Katie butted heads quite a bit about things like that. She would want him to be patient, let people come to things on their own. He always wanted things to happen right then. To his mind, why not if the solution was obvious. Or at least to him, anyway."

"That isn't exactly what I'm used to. I wasn't raised that way," Clara said, thinking of the respect she had for her parents and brother and that they had for her. Any decisions had been made as a family, and when they did not agree, accommodations were made for each one to be happy.

"No, neither were we," Sadie said. "Maybe why we were all such good friends."

"Ah, that explains a lot," Tripp said as he smiled at his wife. "Hard-headed, but respectful, too." His smile turned to a laugh as she blushed and nudged him with her elbow.

"Is Hank like that, too? I know you were raised in that house and you don't strike me that way." Clara turned to Tripp as she rubbed her eyes.

"I don't think Hank and I are that way. We always take into consideration how other people feel." Tripp put his arm around Sadie as he spoke.

Sadie let out an exaggerated cough as her eyes grew wide and she looked at her husband. "Tripp Morgan, I had to practically beat you over the head with a copper pot to get your attention."

"Oh, right." Tripp looked down sheepishly. "Well, if Hank and I are alike in that way, then I can assure you that it is not malicious."

"Dunderheaded, maybe, but not malicious," Suzanne added as she glanced at James. "Either way, it appears that Clara needs a little more time to find out for herself."

"There is nothing at all wrong with waiting a while, Clara. You have nothing to feel bad about. That was truly poor form, what Mr. Archer did." Sadie poured boiling water into the teapot as they sat at her kitchen table.

"I agree, Clara. We will support whatever you decide, and you are welcome to stay here as long as you like," James said as he ushered Tripp out the door.

"No question about it. And to not even tell Hank? Who could imagine?" Suzanne said as she came through the door after putting the twins to bed.

"Honestly, we all knew this was coming. And it appears that there's a timeline on the inheritance." Clara picked up the spoon on the table and turned it over and over in her hand.

"Well, it was thoughtless, at best. He should know any decent girl would want to at least have a say in her wedding. I mean, he has six daughters. If he doesn't know that, he needs to." Suzanne pushed herself away from the table, sending her chair scooting behind her. Pouring the tea into mugs, she set one down in front of Sadie and Clara.

Sadie poured some cream into her cup, gently taking the spoon from Clara and stirring her tea. "Clara, what is it that you want. This is your wedding. How do you want it to be?"

Clara propped her elbows on the table and rested her chin in her hands. She sighed, shaking her head, and said, "I don't exactly know. But I just felt that it wasn't right. Not for me. Not for Hank. I've felt since I met him, and even more so when I met his family, that there are some things that are unhappy at that house."

Sadie blew on her tea and took a sip. "Do you mean bad things? Tripp and James think the world of the Archers. And I have known Hank to be very kind and cordial. And he obviously loves his sisters."

"Yes, he does. He was rapt with attention during their song, and it was a nice gift. At least they thought it was a wedding gift." Clara warmed her hands on her tea, wishing she had a clear answer to her dilemma.

Suzanne stood and put the cream back into the icebox, taking a piece of apple pie out and setting it on the table with three forks.

Sadie wiggled her eyebrows at her sister and took a bite of the pie. "This will make everything better," she said, laughing.

"As always," Suzanne said, sitting down and grabbing a fork. "So, Clara, we know that we think Hank is a nice man. Are you having second thoughts?"

Clara had lost her appetite and fiddled with the fork in her hands. "No, I don't think so. I have to say, I think he's very handsome. He seems to smile a lot—at least when he's not around his dad— and I love his laugh lines. And those eyes…"

Sadie slapped her hand on the table. "I knew it. You like him," she said as she and Suzanne both laughed and Clara's cheeks flushed.

"So then what's the problem?" Suzanne took another bite of the pie that was rapidly disappearing.

Clara breathed deeply and sighed. "I think I need to just be there a little more. Understand what is there that is unspoken. It's something, and once I know what it is, I'll know what to do."

"Well, you always have been one to go with your instincts, Clara." Sadie picked up the empty plate and set it next to the sink. She turned around and leaned against the counter, folding her arms. "So, how are you going to do this? To get to know better what's going on?"

Suzanne snapped her fingers. "I know. We all left in such a hurry—and I'm sure glad we did—but you were already in the buggy when the twins said goodbye to Hank. He looked so upset, it was awful."

"I know. With all the ruckus, I didn't even get to say goodbye," Clara said, rubbing her forehead. "That's not what I wanted to happen."

Suzanne reached over and patted Clara's hand. "There is no way to have done things differently with that big surprise he pulled. But as I was saying, Hank told the girls that since everything went south today, they could come back tomorrow and take a short ride. I say you come with us."

"Hey," Sadie said. "Not fair. Tripp and I have to work tomorrow at the restaurant. We'll miss all the good stuff." Her bottom lip stuck out and she pulled an exaggerated frown.

Clara laughed. "I hope there's not a lot that would be worth missing. At least not a big show."

"Like today." Suzanne folded the dishtowel and laid it on the counter.

"Yes, like today." Clara stood and hugged Suzanne and then Sadie. "Thanks for helping me think this through. I can't even imagine being in this situation without you two."

Suzanne and Sadie squeezed her hands. "You don't ever have to be without us again," Sadie said. "We'll figure this out together."

Clara's eyelids drooped and Suzanne took her by the elbow, turning her toward the door. "I think this has been a pretty big day for you, Clara. Why don't you get some sleep and I'll tell Tripp and James the plan?"

"Yes, we can explain. And we'll make arrangements for you to go with the twins for a riding lesson tomorrow, too," Sadie said as she followed them through the door.

"I think you're right. It's the only plan that makes any sense, and I am just exhausted." Clara rubbed her eyes and for the second day in a row, exhaustion swept over her.

"Please, just get a good night's sleep. We can talk more in the morning. And Clara, I'm sorry about today. I had no idea..."

Clara smiled at her friends as she started up the stairs. "I don't think anybody did but Mr. Archer and the few people he did tell. It will be interesting to see what he does next."

Chapter Eight

A fitful night's sleep had resulted in Clara feeling anxious all morning, and when the time came for them to go to the ranch, she'd almost changed her mind and stayed back.

But there was something about Hank—something about that house, that family—that drew her to it. Suzanne had been right. She did like Hank and wanted to know more about him. The only way to do that would be to spend time with him, so she got in the buggy behind Suzanne and they headed toward the ranch, the twins sitting between them.

Beau Archer had gone into Tucson to see his attorney, Rosemary informed them when they arrived at Archer Ranch, and Clara breathed a sigh of relief.

"Hank's at the barn and said for you to go on down when you got here," she said as she eyed Clara warily.

Clara had made it a point to smile and be as unthreatening as she could, but it wasn't working so far.

Suzanne raised her eyebrows at Clara and nodded toward the door, grabbing the twins' hands. "Thank you, Rosemary. We'll just head that way,"

"Goodness, what did I do to her?" Clara asked as she shut the door behind her. "You'd think I'd stolen her boyfriend...oh. They don't want to lose him."

"They sure do look up to their big brother. That may be a part of it, if they think you're taking him away. I guess that's not too unusual."

Suzanne laughed as the twins broke away from her, running at full speed as they spotted Hank down by the barn.

"Be careful, girls. I'll be right there." Suzanne looped her arm through Clara's and tugged at her bonnet. "This should be interesting. The last time, I think Hank was exhausted after his experience with them. Maybe this time will be a little less...frantic."

"Frantic?" Clara tugged at her own bonnet,

wondering if her unruly, red hair was behaving and staying tucked underneath.

"Well, you know the girls are lively, and they really kept him on his toes. I must say, though, he was great with them. He made sure they were safe and followed his directions. Just watch and see what you think."

Hank had each girl by the hand and walked through the barn, horses on each side of him in their stalls. Clara stopped for a moment, listening as each horse gave a soft neigh as he passed. She shook her head, thinking of the horses in Chicago and how she'd heard the same from them.

"Uncle Hank, I want to ride this horse," Lucy said, breaking away and trying to reach the nose of a very large, brown horse who intently watched Hank's movements.

Hank picked her up so she could stroke the horse's nose and said, "Lucy, this is Tracker. He's bigger than ten of you put together. He's very nice, but I think we need to find somebody a little smaller."

"Here's one smaller," Lucy said as he put her down, sending her running to the opposite of the barn.

Lily stood in the middle of the barn, looking from one row of stalls to the other. "Uncle Hank, can I ride one of these over here?" She pointed to the bank of stalls on the side that Tracker was on.

Hank raised his eyebrows and bent down to Lily. "And why would that be, Lily?"

"I...I don't know. I just like these better."

Lucy came over and said, "Yeah. They're prettier."

"Ah, prettier. Well, on this side of the barn are horses I broke. The other side—those horses I don't know so well."

Lucy's eyes flew wide open. "You broke horses? Why, Uncle Hank? That's not nice," she said as she folded her arms over her small chest.

Hank's laugh sent a warmth through Clara that surprised her. He reached down and tugged on Lucy's braid as he walked further along. "Not that kind of broke, Lucy. Breaking a horse means something different. And different things to different people," he said as he stroked the nose of each horse he passed by. "It really means teaching them how to do what they need to do."

"Oh, good. I wouldn't want the horses to be hurt," Lily said, putting her hand in Hank's.

"Neither would I, Lily," he said, squeezing the little one's hand.

Clara and Suzanne followed behind along the bank of stalls that Lily had chosen and stroked the noses of several of the horses as she passed by.

"Don't horses frighten you, Clara? I mean, I can handle horses that I know, but some of them are pretty unpredictable, and sometimes they make me nervous.

They both jumped as one of the horses behind them, on the opposite side of the barn, kicked the door holding him in and reared his head, neighing loudly.

"Like that?" Clara said, reflexively taking a step backward, away from the horse.

"Yes, like that. They're so very big and could really hurt somebody."

"I have to say I haven't been around too many, but no, I've not felt afraid. Somehow, I feel very calm around them."

Hank looked up and smiled as Suzanne and

Clara made it to where he was with the girls. He stood, wiping his hands on his pants and tipping his hat. "Hello, Clara, Suzanne. Nice to see you."

Hank replaced his hat quickly, but not before Clara could see his ears flush, and she smiled behind her hand.

"I'm mighty sorry about yesterday, Clara. I had no idea that was going to happen, and Pa and I had some pretty strong words after you left." Hank passed the twins back to Suzanne as he opened one of the stall doors, his head down.

Suzanne's gaze caught Clara's and she batted her eyelashes, making Clara laugh. "Hank, how about I take the girls out to the arena and we wait for you to saddle up?"

"Huh?" he said, turning back to Suzanne. "Oh, that would be great. I'll have the horse saddled up in a minute and I'll meet you out there."

He looked quickly at Clara and then turned back to the horse, a beautiful white one, brushing it in long strokes. As he set the brush down and reached for the saddle blanket, Clara said, "Hank, I'd like to apologize, too, for our abrupt departure. I'm afraid I was just so surprised that I didn't know what to do. I'd been looking forward to talking with you later, and that just took me completely by surprise."

Hank chuckled grimly, shaking his head. "You and me both. I had no idea that was going to happen. I would have stopped it if I had."

"I can see why he would be in a rush—I think. It is your property, isn't it?"

Hank shook his head slowly. "Yes, it's supposed to be. And yes, there is a timeline, but it's another couple of weeks out, so there's a bit of time to let you make sure this is what you want. I'm mighty grateful you're even considering it."

He nodded at her as he threw the saddle on the horse and tightened the leather straps beneath its belly.

"I'd like to get to know you better, Hank, but I'm more than willing to consider it."

He threw his head back and his deep, rich laugh made her skin tingle. She wondered if he could sing, too, like his sisters.

"Well, if you're still interested after that fiasco, you're pretty courageous."

"I don't scare easily, Mr. Archer, but I do have my limits."

He leaned over the back of the horse, his eyes intent on hers. "All joking aside, Clara, I really would like to get to know you, too. Would you join me for dinner tonight? I'd like to take you out."

"Oh," she said, the butterflies returning after a lengthy absence when they'd been replaced by worry. "That would be lovely, Hank."

He smiled broadly, his white teeth flashing in his tanned face. "Thank you, Clara. We'll have a chance to talk, then. Can I fetch you at six o'clock?"

"Yes, thank you. That's perfect," she said as she left the stall.

Hank finished saddling the horse, the bridle in place. "By the way, this here is Regalo."

"Regalo?" she asked, running her hand down its smooth nose. "He's beautiful."

"Yes, he is."

She thought she saw his face cloud yet again as he pulled his hat further down his forehead. He led the young horse in the direction Suzanne and the girls had gone.

She followed him, stopping short as she rounded the corner behind him. In front of her stood a large, fenced arena with benches placed on one side under a stand of trees. Suzanne and the girls sat in the shade, Lucy and Lily jumping up as soon as they saw Hank heading in their direction.

Clara sat down beside Suzanne as Hank lifted Lily into the saddle and placed her hands tightly on the saddle horn. He walked beside her as he guided Regalo into the arena, slowly leading him around the fence line in a big circle.

"Lily doesn't look too sure about this," Clara said, squinting to see Lily on the other side of the arena.

Suzanne pulled at her sleeve and bounced her knee as she watched Lily round the final curve. "No, she's not near as wild about it as Lucy. She always thinks it's a great idea until it's time to actually get on the horse. Probably what I would do, too."

Lucy's had her nose up to the fence and was hooting and hollering her sister's name as she rounded the arena and came closer.

Hank stopped, holding the reins to his side and wrapping his arm around Lily's back, her knuckles white as she clung to the saddle. He bent and whispered something in her ear, and Clara's heart warmed to see her smile and lighten her grip on the saddle just a little.

"Lucy, remember what I told you about yelling so much when Regalo comes by? He's just new to this and we don't want to scare him."

Hank caught Suzanne's eye and she walked over to Lucy, grabbing her hand and pulling her onto her lap as she sat on one of the benches. "Let's just quietly wave as they come by," she said.

Lucy waved frantically—but silently—as Lily passed by on Regalo, looking a bit more relaxed. They circled the arena one more time before Lily turned to Hank and said, "Can I be done now?"

Hank chuckled and lifted her down off the horse, flipping his reins through the fence and walking her over to Suzanne. "You can be done any time you want, little one."

Lily ran to her mother and buried her face in her skirts as Suzanne smoothed her hair. "You were very brave, Lily. Mama's proud of you," she said gently.

"Come on, Lucy, your turn," Hank called, patting the saddle as she ran over, her arms raised to be lifted up and a smile from ear to ear.

"Interesting they're so different, isn't it," Clara said. She watched Lucy bounce up and down on the saddle as Hank whispered to her. Lucy turned to him, his eyes never leaving her as she settled onto the horse and calmly finished her two trips around the arena.

"They sure are. I'm so glad that Hank has such a good way with both of them. Look how fast Lucy calmed down. She doesn't normally settle that quickly with anybody—besides you," she said, turning to Clara and smiling.

"Oh," Clara said, surprised. "I didn't know that. But he does have a way with them both."

As they circled around the arena the second time, Hank looked up and smiled, waving in their direction. "Oh, look, he's waving at you," Suzanne said.

"Me? He's not waving at me." Again, those butterflies that seemed to have taken up residence in her stomach fluttered.

"Well, he's not waving at Lily," Suzanne said as she pointed to Lily who had fallen fast asleep on her lap.

They stood as Hank tied Regalo to the arena fence and walked Lucy over to the benches.

"Mama, that was so fun. I want to do that every day." Lucy jumped up and down, tugging at Hank.

"We'll see, little one. I think I heard I'm heading out on the trail pretty soon so it'll have to wait until I get back." He stood up and tousled her hair.

"Another cattle drive?" Suzanne asked as she walked with the girls toward where the buggy was tied up.

Hank took off his hat and rubbed the back of his neck, his forehead wrinkling in a frown. "I'm afraid so. After Pa and I had our...er...discussion last night about the wedding, he told me that we should be heading out in not too long."

"Maybe that's why he was in such a hurry," Clara said as she helped the girls into the buggy and climbed up behind them.

"No, I don't think so. I mean, sure, he'd want us to get married before I go, but I don't think he's considered that it might be difficult for you here all alone if I did head out with the crew on the drive. Not the sort of thing that he'd think about. Not anymore, anyway," Hank said, pulling his hat back on and glancing up to the house.

"Girls, thank Uncle Hank for taking you on a ride today," Suzanne said as she climbed in the buggy and took the reins that Hank handed her.

"Thank you, Uncle Hank," the girls chorused, waving frantically from the buggy.

Hank smiled and tipped his hat to them. "It was my pleasure, ladies. Anytime I can oblige, I'd be more than happy to. And it was very nice to see you again, Clara," he said, his laugh lines crinkling as he smiled up at her. "I look forward to seeing you tonight."

Clara's cheeks blushed as he backed up, giving Suzanne room to get the horses moving. He'd turned the buggy around already and they were all situated to head home so she headed down the drive, the twins waving until Hank was no longer in sight.

"Tonight?" Suzanne asked, her eyebrows wiggling up and down as she looked at Clara.

"Stop. It's just dinner. He asked me out to dinner, that's all."

"Can we go, Mama?" Lucy asked, tugging at her mother's sleeve.

"No, sweetheart. This one's just for grown-ups," she answered, batting her eyelashes again at Clara as she turned out the gate of the Archer Ranch.

Chapter Nine

"These earrings match your eyes perfectly, Clara, and we want you to wear them tonight. They look beautiful with your dress." Suzanne pushed Lily forward and she opened her hand to reveal a pair of stunning emerald earrings. "Unless, of course, you want to wear the pearls your mother gave you. I know how much they mean to you."

Clara took the earrings and stood in front of the mirror, holding them up to her ears. They really did accent her eyes and matched her dress perfectly.

"Oh, thank you, Lily. They're beautiful, and I promise I'll take very good care of them." Turning to Suzanne, she said, "That was very thoughtful of them. I'd like to wear them, if you don't mind. I'm a little nervous—but it feels more like excited. I don't think I need the pearls tonight." She turned in a circle and asked Lily and Lucy, "Do I look all right?"

They ran to hug her and she smoothed their hair as she hugged them in return. Suzanne leaned against the wall, eyeing her friend thoughtfully. "You know, Clara, your hair is so beautiful. With the red waves, it makes your eyes look even more green. He's not going to know what to do when he sees you."

"Yes, Clara. You look like a princess," Lucy added, at which her sister nodded solemnly.

The twins jumped at the knock on the door, racing down the stairs. James met them at the bottom and stopped them with open arms. "Hey, hey, slow down."

"But Daddy, Hank's here and Clara looks like a princess. Mama says he won't know what to do when he sees her, so I wanna see what happens." Lucy hopped from one foot to another as she tried to wriggle away from her father's grasp.

He picked them both up, one under each arm, and laughed as he set them down by the fire. "I think we can watch from here, don't you, Suzanne?"

"Yes, please." She sighed as she and Clara walked down the stairs, James's eyes growing wide at the sight of Clara.

"My goodness," he said as Clara stepped off the bottom step, thinking that her face must be as red as her hair.

"See, Daddy, we told you. A princess," Lucy said as she clapped her hands together.

"Hank's a lucky man," he said as he wrapped his arm around Suzanne's shoulder. "Almost as lucky as I am."

Suzanne laughed and pulled away. "Well, one of us ought to actually open the door."

As Suzanne swung the door open, Clara grasped the newel post to steady herself. She wasn't quite sure why she was nervous—no, excited—and thought maybe it was because she'd never been courted before.

But when she saw Hank's face, his wide eyes and big smile as he saw her, she knew it wasn't just because someone was taking her out to dinner. It was because it was *this* someone.

She looked down and smoothed her dress to break eye contact as she remembered that he was courting her for two reasons, neither of which involved caring about her. His inheritance, and to avoid his father's wrath.

Hank held his hat to his chest and stepped into the room, his eyes still locked on Clara. James and Suzanne exchanged glances and James cleared his throat.

"Oh, hello, James, Suzanne," Hank said, blinking as if suddenly realizing there was anyone else in the room.

Lucy jumped off the settee and ran to Hank, Lily close behind. "Doesn't she look like a princess, Uncle Hank?"

He hugged the girls and looked back up at Clara. "Yes, Lucy, I believe she does."

He stood and wiped his hand on his pants again before extending her his arm. "Shall we go, Clara? I have a reservation waiting for us."

Clara looked at Suzanne, wishing that she knew more about this sort of thing, and received a comforting smile in return. She took a deep breath and decided that whatever was to happen would happen as she threaded her arm through his.

"Thank you, everyone. I'll see you later," Clara said as she let Hank guide her out to the buggy.

"Clara, I must say that you look lovely," Hank said as he helped her into the buggy.

"Thank you, Hank. You look nice yourself," she said, noticing more how he smelled than how he looked. He had on a different clasp on his string tie tonight, all silver, that looked sort of Indian from the pictures in her picture book. Where was that book, anyway?

"Your tie is interesting. Is it Indian?" she asked, peering over at him as he turned the buggy toward town.

"Oh, this? No, not this one. This one is from Mexico. We're so close to the border that there are many things that make an appearance as the cultures mingle."

"We're close to Mexico?" she said, wishing she remembered more from her geography lessons in school. Was that in the book, too?

"Yes," he said, chuckling. "People seem to be surprised by that, but it's not like there's a fence or anything separating us. And we have things they need and vice versa."

"Is that where your father learned about adobe houses?" She tried to look straight ahead as they made small talk, wondering where they were going to and hoping it was to the Occidental.

"I believe partly. He's always been interested in things like that. He has a lot of flaws, especially since my mother passed away, but he's always had great respect for people and the land. That's why this is all so surprising to me, how he's behaving."

Clara cleared her throat, not quite sure what to say. All she knew about Mr. Archer so far was that he was heavy-handed and didn't include his son in important decisions—like his own marriage. So far, she didn't feel like she had much use for him.

"Well, here we are," Hank said as he pulled up to the Occidental and stopped the buggy close to the hitching post. He pointed to a store on the corner. "That next door is James's mercantile. That's where I first met him."

She gazed at the big porch and lovely shutters, and the sign over the door announcing Tripp and Sadie's restaurant.

As Hank came and offered her his hand to help her step out of the buggy, she stood and turned around, marveling at the busy street. She gasped as her heel slipped off the buggy step and she fell backward, closing her eyes and hoping she didn't hit the ground too hard.

Perfect. My first ever evening out with a man and I...

Her heart thudded in her chest as she awaited the impact with the dirt, but time stopped as she felt strong arms break her fall. She opened her eyes finally, gratefully looking up into those of Hank.

Her mortification subsided as he laughed, and said, "Well, that was…not the most graceful thing I've ever seen."

She smiled as his eyes twinkled, and she held her hand to her forehead in mock horror and said, "What else is a princess to do when her foot slips out from under her. Thank you for saving me."

Hank set her down, taking her hand and bowing before her. "It was an honor, my lady." He held his arm out for her, and she slipped hers in and let him guide her into the restaurant.

"Clara. Hank," she heard the minute they entered the beautiful dining room of the Occidental.

Sadie rushed to them and grabbed Clara's

hand, pulling her to the best table in the house. "Here, I saved the table with the best view out the window for you."

Clara's heart tugged at her friend's excitement, grateful that everyone seemed to be cheering them on and hoping for the best.

Hank pulled out her chair for her and scooted her in as he smiled at Sadie. "Is Tripp in the kitchen?" he asked, looking over toward the door.

"Yes, and he's busy right now, but I'm sure he'll be out soon to say hello." She smiled and offered them both menus, turning and pointing over to a beautiful, mahogany bar that spanned the length of the room. "And we have a bartender finally. We were able to open the bar for people to wait for an open table. Tripp says it's someone you know, Hank. Name's Samuel something."

"Samuel Ford? Really?" Hank stood and looked over to the bar. "Well, I'll be. I haven't seen him for years. Clara, mind if I say hello real quick?" he said as he placed his hat on the chair beside him.

"Oh, no, please go ahead." She unfolded her napkin and laid it in her lap as Sadie quickly sat in Hank's chair.

"So, how is everything?" she whispered as Hank walked toward the bar and extended his hand to the man behind it. He was greeted with a broad smile and sturdy handshake from the tall, lean man in a satin vest and white shirt, his sleeves rolled up.

"I think all right, but I almost fell out of the buggy. Hank had to catch me," Clara said, fanning herself with her menu.

"How romantic," Sadie said with a sigh. "You know, I think you two are perfect for each other, Beau Archer notwithstanding. Uh-oh, speak of the devil." Sadie stood and turned as Beau Archer strode through the room, taking a quick glance at his son at the bar and heading straight for Clara.

"Hello, Mr. Archer. Nice to see you," Sadie said as she raised her eyebrows at Clara. "Are you here for supper?"

"No, no, thank you, Sadie. I've just returned from Tucson with some news, and would like to speak with Miss Martin quickly for a moment, if you don't mind." He held Clara's gaze and didn't glance at Sadie.

"Oh, well, if that's okay with Clara..." Sadie

stood for a moment, shifting her feet as Clara contemplated her potential future father-in-law.

"Thank you, Sadie. I'm sure we'll be fine." She gestured for Mr. Archer to take Hank's seat as she stole a glance at him laughing at the bar with his friend.

Beau glanced at Hank as well before he cleared his throat, pausing for a moment.

Clara waited, wondering what he could possibly have to say to her. Somehow, she didn't think she'd be getting an apology.

Beau took a deep breath and sat back in his chair. "Clara, I can imagine that this is a little difficult for you. I'd like to first thank you for even considering helping us in this complicated situation."

Clara folded her arms and leveled her gaze at Hank's father. "You're welcome." She fell silent, waiting for him to continue and enjoying his obvious discomfort, despite herself.

"I believe that you are aware that my wife, Hank and the girls' mother, passed away not too long ago. Actually, she was Tripp's mother, too. At least, she considered herself to be."

Clara dropped her hands to the table as she looked down at her napkin. "Yes, I did know that, Mr. Archer. I'm sorry for your loss."

"Thank you," he said with a glance down at the table. "It is imperative that this property becomes Hanks as soon as possible. It is what his mother would have wanted."

Clara frowned as she wondered what Mrs. Archer had to do with anything regarding the property. She recalled that it had belonged to Katie's father, but knew nothing beyond that.

She sighed, leaning forward on her elbows. "Mr. Archer, I understand that this is meaningful to you. It would be impossible to miss that fact."

He smiled, steepling his fingers in front of him as he assessed Clara from across the table.

"Miss Martin, yes, you are correct. It is very important to me, and it would be to Hank if he knew all of the facts."

"I'm sure that Hank is as aware that this is important to you as I am, but I'm not at all sure why. Maybe you should…"

She stole another glance at Hank, just as he turned and spotted his father at the table with her.

His face reddened and he quickly said something to his friend before striding over to the table.

"Pa, what are you doing here?" he asked, glaring down at his father.

"Nothing, Hank. Nothing, really. Just having a quick word with your future bride." He stood, moving away from Hank's seat and gestured for him to take it.

"Thank you," Hank said as he sat across from Clara, casting a sideways glance at his father.

Beau remained in place, thoughtful during the awkward silence that followed. He seemed to make a decision, and cleared his throat.

"Could I convince the two of you to take a ride with me tomorrow? To see the property?"

"What? I've seen it, Pa. Not sure Clara's even interested," Hank said, studying his father.

"Now, Hank, you've seen part of it. There's something particular I'd like to show you. I can have the housekeeper pack a picnic. I'll show you what I want you to see, and head back. You two can stay and roam around as you like."

"Pa, I don't know..." Hank looked across the

table to Clara, his eyebrows raised, waiting for her response.

Clara looked from Hank to his father, and made a decision. She wanted to clear up as much of this confusion as possible, and if it took a ride out to the property to do that, so be it. She needed to know…to move on.

"That would be fine with me, Mr. Archer. I would be happy to come along. Maybe Hank will even give me a riding lesson like he did for the twins today." She smiled at Hank as he looked up at his father.

Hank sighed. "How is eleven o'clock? Pa, I really need to know what this is all about. Clara deserves to know, too."

Beau's head dropped into his hand and he rubbed his eyes. "Hank, thank you for trusting me. I think tomorrow, after we go to the property, you may understand a little better."

He turned to Clara, bowing slightly toward her. "And thank you, Miss Martin, for humoring me. I look forward to seeing you tomorrow."

With a quick nod to Hank, Beau turned and left the restaurant.

Almost as if on cue—not that she would have been listening—Sadie came to the table. "Everything okay?"

Clara smiled at Hank, happy that tomorrow, she'd finally find out what the urgency was about the property. Not the timeline, but what it meant to Beau—to the family.

"Yes, we're fine, Sadie. Everything is great."

Sadie sighed as she let out a deep breath. "Oh, good. Are you ready to order?"

Chapter Ten

Hank turned his gaze back to Clara as Sadie went into the kitchen to give Tripp their order.

"I'm sorry about that with my father. Was it all right? Did he say anything—"

She held her hands up to stop him. "Don't worry, Hank. He was actually quite polite. And interesting. He thanked me for being here, actually, and considering your proposition."

Hank dropped the spoon he'd been turning over in his hand and sighed. "Oh, that's a relief. When I saw him here with you, I didn't know what to think. Worried me."

Her curiosity got the better of her and she picked up her glass of water, attempting to appear nonchalant as she asked, "Oh? Why?"

Hank picked up the spoon again, twisting it in his hand. "Yesterday didn't actually go so well, even after you left. I'm not sure what's going on, and I didn't want him to upset you. I want this to go well, and I don't understand why he's doing this at all."

He stared at the spoon as it spun. She leaned forward, gently taking it from his hand and setting it on the table, encouraging him to meet her eyes. She felt his anxiety and concern, and wanted him to relax and have a nice evening.

"I'm a big girl, Hank. I very much appreciate your concern for me, but so far, he hasn't dished out anything I can't take."

His look of relief warmed her heart, and she smiled as he reached over and placed his hand on hers. "Thank you. You are more kind than we deserve. I hope that tomorrow will explain some of his behavior."

"I hope so. I..." Clara set her water glass down and cleared her throat, preparing herself to ask the question she'd wanted to ask since she'd arrived. When the time came, though, the words wouldn't pass her lips.

Hank cocked his head, his confusion clear. "Yes?" he asked, patiently waiting for her to continue.

She shook her head. She didn't really know this man—it was premature to ask when he thought he wanted to be married. So far, he'd seemed content to let her decide, but she'd seen him enough times now to know that while he was concerned over his father's recent actions, he also was strong and capable of deciding things for himself. His actions to protect her the previous day from his father had shown her that.

She decided to hold her tongue about an actual wedding date, and instead asked, "How long have you been riding the trail? Cattle drives, is it?"

Hank sat back in his chair, rubbing his forehead. "Too long. Much too long. It was exciting for a while—quite a while."

He picked up the spoon again and started to spin it but looked up to see Clara's smile and put it back down with a laugh.

"But after watching Tripp go away to chef school and come back and make a nice life for himself, I'm feeling more and more that I want that, too."

Clara looked up at the copper tiles on the ceiling and soaked in the warm ambiance of the dining room. Sadie caught her eye and winked, attending to another table.

"They seem to have done something remarkable in a relatively short period of time." She turned back to Hank and frowned as he leaned forward and looked down at his place setting, his arms resting against the table.

"Thing is, we've been doing it this way at the ranch for so long, not sure Pa will have it any other way. Tripp's path was different and he had to go. I, on the other hand, have run the drives for so long, I don't think my father thinks I can do anything else." He rubbed his chin and sat back in his chair.

She regarded him for a bit, her heart tugging at the frustration in his voice. "It's no longer something that you love, is that it?"

He shook his head slowly. "It's not only that. Yes, it's challenging to sleep on the ground, and the older I get, the more I appreciate a soft bed."

He looked up quickly, blushing as he realized what he'd just said. "Oh, I'm sorry," he said. "I didn't mean to—"

Clara laughed at his discomfort and said, "Oh, Hank, no apology necessary. I believe we've all seen and slept in beds before. And I'm not nearly that delicate as to not be able to speak of it."

She appreciated his sensibility but was amused by it. She wondered if he'd courted before, and was pretty sure that with all of his cattle drives, he'd been too busy, just like she'd been.

His forehead smoothed as the frown left his face, the laugh lines returning, much to her relief.

"Thank you for that," he said as Sadie approached with their meals.

"Roast chicken for you, Clara, and for Hank, his favorite. Beef stew—although with red wine. Not exactly like the trail." She set down a basket of biscuits and said, "Let me know if you need anything else, and enjoy."

"It must be very good beef stew for him to serve it in the restaurant."

Hank bent over his bowl and inhaled deeply, his eyes closed and a look of delight spreading over his face. "Yes, it is. It's the best I've ever had. I'm so glad that Tripp decided to put it on the menu."

Clara inhaled the delicious aroma of the chicken she'd ordered and her stomach grumbled. "Oh, goodness. I do apologize." She laughed, holding her hand over her belly. "I guess I'm hungry, and this just pushed me over the edge."

Hank's eyes twinkled. "Don't apologize to me, either. I love to eat, and a woman with a good appetite is something I've always..."

Clara looked up at him, her fork stopping mid-air as she watched his eyes twinkle but his ears turn pink.

"...Appreciated. Truly. My mother was a fabulous cook, and eating was always highly encouraged at my house." His eyes softened as he took a wistful glance around the room.

"She would have loved this." Hank folded his napkin in his lap and turned his blue eyes back to Clara. "I sure wish you could have met her."

Clara placed her hand over Hank's, his sadness pulling at her heart. "It seems that you all miss her very much. No doubt she was a wonderful lady to have been so well-loved."

"Yes, we all miss her, but I think Pa more than anyone, if you can imagine. They met and married so young, and truly in a whirlwind."

She waited, silently encouraging him to continue, pleased that she was getting a little more information.

"Pa hasn't been the same since she passed away, and the girls are having a difficult time. But I'm away so much, I can't to a darn thing about it. Not that he'd talk about it anyway. He's not like that."

He looked up at Sadie as she delivered a big piece of chocolate cake and set it between them. She cleared their dinner plates and set down a fork in front of each of them.

"It's the last piece. You'll have to share," she said as she winked at Clara.

Hank cleared his throat as Sadie walked away. "Is that all right with you?"

The thought crossed her mind fleetingly that it might not be appropriate to share food with someone who was courting her, but since no one had ever told her if there were rules, she decided that it sounded just fine to her.

"Of course it is," she said as she picked up her fork and cut a piece of cake. She closed her eyes as it melted in her mouth. Sadie truly was the best baker she'd ever known.

"You feel, then, that if you were able to leave

the trail things might actually be better for your father?"

Hank nodded as he took a bite of the cake. "Yes, I do. There's quite a bit to do, running a ranch, and he's got that on top of taking care of the girls—who can be a handful, as you may have surmised."

"Ah, yes, it appeared that way. So, although you have a housekeeper, you'd like to be more involved with the business of running the ranch rather than the physical aspects of the cattle drive?"

"That's it, exactly. I've learned a thing or two that might be helpful around the ranch, and we don't necessarily need to put all our time and energy into cattle drives, anyway." He finished abruptly, almost as if he'd said something he shouldn't have, and he glanced around quickly at the other patrons.

"Oh?" Clara's interest was piqued and she remembered how much Hank had seemed to enjoy being with the twins.

He leaned forward and lowered his voice. "Yes, there are things that we could do that would be more beneficial, but Pa won't hear of it. Says this is the way it's always been and will continue to be."

Clara set her fork down and dabbed at her mouth with her napkin, watching Hank as he finished the last bit of cake. "Maybe once we get to the bottom of this property issue, other options might come up that he would be willing to consider?"

Hank sighed and shook his head. "I've tried. So far, with no luck."

"Well, you can't give up, Hank. If you say there are other things that can be done, you should be allowed the opportunity to do them. Right is right."

Hank's eyes twinkled. "Right is right? I agree with you, but sometimes there are things standing in the way. Maybe tomorrow we'll find out more."

Clara smiled, anxious to be on the lookout the following day for any information that might help Hank on his quest to change his life. She already had some thoughts forming as Hank signaled to Sadie for the check.

Chapter Eleven

When Clara awoke the next morning, it took her a moment to get her bearings. So much had happened in a few short days that if she wasn't careful, her head would reel and she might just go to New York. She'd never considered that she might be under the thumb of an overbearing father-in-law.

She smiled, though, as she realized that she didn't want to leave yet. Today was the day she'd find out what some of these mysteries were about, and her instincts told her that it was important for her to find out—for her *and* Hank.

A red cardinal settled on her windowsill as she sat up and stretched. She watched it as it fluttered its wings in the morning sun. It flew away as she went to the window and she smiled as it danced in the birdbath that Suzanne and the girls filled up every day, joyously watching the birds come and go.

She drew in a sharp breath when she splashed her face with the cold water in the washbasin. Pulling her nightdress over her head, she dressed, quickly braided her hair and made her bed, smoothing her hand over the comforter as she looked around her comfortable room.

A flash of red drew her eye to the cardinal sitting on the windowsill again. Her hands fiddled with the cameo at her neck as her forehead rested on the cool glass. Remembering her conversation with Mr. Archer the previous night, she sincerely hoped that their trip to the property today would shed some light on this whole subject—maybe enough that she could decide if a wedding was in order.

Her hand on the doorknob, she stopped and turned around, moving in front of the vanity. She placed several of the lavender flowers in her braid and behind her ear, enjoying the scent as she thought of the new experience she'd have today.

As she headed down the stairs, she realized that since she'd decided to come to Arizona Territory, everything had been a series of new experiences, just as she'd hoped. Even though they didn't always turn out the way she wanted, each one gave her another piece of the puzzle that was her new family, and drew her closer to making a decision.

It was that sense of promise she carried with her as she rode with Hank in his buggy, away from town and toward Archer Ranch. "Thank you for agreeing to do this, Clara. It really is above and beyond, but it seems to mean a great deal to my father. He seemed very nervous this morning. Was doing a lot of pacing."

"He was?" she asked, surprised. He'd always seemed calm and in control to her, and she wondered again what was making him so agitated.

"The property line is adjacent to that of the ranch, but it's very big, so we'll head up into about the middle. We used to come here when we were little, but I haven't been in a long time. I do remember there were some pretty fine views."

He guided the buggy on what looked to her to be a road—well, just wagon-wheel ruts—that hadn't been used much for a very long time. Hoof prints preceded them and Hank followed along in silence while she took in the scenery.

She'd asked Suzanne for the picture book

before she left, and she flipped through the pages, comparing drawings of plants and trees in the book to the real things in front of her.

Hank had laughed when he'd seen the book, asking, "What is that? The tourist's guide to Arizona Territory? Didn't know there was one of those things."

She nudged him with her elbow as she continued to flip the pages. "If I'm going to live somewhere new, I want to know all about it."

"You think you want to live here, do you?" he said quietly, peering at her out of the corner of his eye.

She took in a quick breath, surprised at the warmth that spread through her chest at his question. She looked up at him, her eyes soft as she said, "I just think I might, Hank Archer. I just might."

As they'd risen toward the small hill in the center of the property, the vegetation had changed and Clara could barely keep up with it, looking things up in her book.

Beau Archer's voice boomed from atop a small rise amid a stand of tall trees. "Hello. Up here."

Hank and Clara both looked up, shielding their eyes from the sun.

"What's he doing up there?" Hank asked under his breath.

"I don't know. Have you been up there before?"

"No, we never came anywhere this far in. Stayed down at the stream where we turned in, mostly. Wonder what he's up to."

"Can't wait to find out," Clara muttered as she clapped the book closed and pushed it under her seat.

Hank pulled the buggy up next to Beau's horse. After he tied the horses to the tree, he helped Clara hop down and said, "Looks like he walked up there. You okay with that?"

"Of course." She turned toward the road they'd come up. The view over the valley and toward the west, the mountains rising behind her, almost took her breath away. "Oh, Hank, it's beautiful here."

"It is, isn't it? I can only imagine what it looks like from up there. We can probably see Tombstone." He reached for her hand, pulling her along as he headed to where his father stood, looking quietly over the valley.

Hank kept hold of her hand as she lifted her skirts with the other so she didn't trip over the rocks that were getting bigger as they climbed. As the smaller rocks turned to boulders, closer to the side of the hill, he turned to check on her. "You all right?"

"Only a little further," Beau shouted as they rounded a huge boulder.

Clara hit her forehead on Hank's back as he stopped short in front of her. Rubbing it, she peeked around Hank and stood, as frozen to the spot as he was.

In the clearing ahead of them stood a small, white house with vivid blue window frames, what appeared to Clara to be a duplicate of the small house at the ranch, the one with the failing garden.

"Come ahead, son. This is what I wanted to show you," Beau said quietly as he turned and started toward the door.

Hank gripped Clara's hand again and slowly followed his father, pulling her along behind him. As they reached the door, Beau took off his hat and held it over his heart, looking up and around the house as he rubbed the back of his neck with his handkerchief.

He took a deep breath and seemed to make a decision, reaching for the handle of the door and pushing it open. He disappeared into the house after beckoning for them to follow.

Hank turned to Clara, his eyes narrowing with concern. "You want to do this? You don't have to if you don't want to."

She nodded slowly and looked from Hank to his father, who stood again in the doorway, his hands on his hips as he impatiently waited for them.

As Clara's eyes adjusted to the darkness inside the house, Beau moved from window to window, opening curtains as dust flew everywhere. She held her handkerchief to her mouth as Hank held his sleeve over his own.

Beau walked around the house slowly, picking up items as he moved along the walls. She watched as he lifted a tortoise-shell mirror off a small vanity and held it to his heart as he bowed his head.

He placed it carefully back down and looked around the single room once more before heading back to the door, placing his hands on each side of the doorframe as he looked over the view behind them.

Hank dropped Clara's hand and moved to the vanity. He reached for a small, framed photograph and studied the black and white image of a very young woman who looked vaguely familiar.

Beau turned as Hank set it back on the vanity.

"Mama?" Hank said, his voice quiet.

Clara lifted a dust-filled cloth off of what looked like a settee and sat, not wanting to interrupt.

Beau returned to the vanity and placed his arm around Hank's shoulders.

"Yes, son. Mama."

Hank rubbed his eyes before he looked over to his father. "I don't understand. What is this place, Pa? Why haven't you ever shown us before?"

Beau sighed, running his finger over the framed photograph of his wife. He cleared his throat, wiping his shirtsleeve over his forehead as he turned and walked out the door. "Come on out here and I'll tell you."

Hank reached for Clara's hand, helping her up and ushering her out the door. Beau had sat on the wide front porch in a swing built for two.

Hank pulled a chair up for Clara as he leaned against the porch's bannister, folding his arms over his chest as he watched his father gaze out over the horizon.

"Son," Hank's father started, his voice low and quiet. "I think you probably know how hard it's been for me since your mother passed away. She was the love of my life, and we had many happy years together. Built the ranch up together from nothing, and raised a fine family."

"Yes, Pa, you did."

"You also know your mother was the talker in the family, the sensitive one. Always told me to just keep my mouth shut when it came to matters of the heart and that she would look out for me," he said with a small chuckle at the memory. "She knew what was for my own good. And yours, too."

"That was probably best," Hank said as he smiled and walked to Beau, resting his hand on his father's shoulder.

Beau gave his hand a quick pat before he stood

and walked to the bannister, leaning on it and looking out over the valley below.

"I know you don't remember your grandfather, but he loved your mother very much. It was me he wasn't too wild about." Beau turned and leaned against the bannister, looking from Hank to Clara. "He and his wife, your grandmother, lived in town with your mother, and when I came in at the end of a cattle drive and got one look at her walking down the street with her parents, it was all over for me."

Clara sighed, the romantic image warming her heart. "Did you marry right away, Mr. Archer?" She was curious to learn how long a courtship they'd had.

"No, although that would have been fine with me. Took me a few more cattle drives and proving myself to your grandpa before he'd let me anywhere near her."

He smiled, and Clara got a glimpse of the same twinkle she'd seen in Hank's eyes.

"What does this house have to do with anything?"

"Well, he'd owned this property for quite a

while, had intended to build a house up here for him and your grandmother. She was a little delicate, and couldn't be this far out of town. So when I announced my intentions for your mother's hand in marriage, he took me to the saloon, bought me a whiskey and we made a deal."

"A deal?" Hank's eyebrows rose as he plopped down on the swing where his father had sat.

"Yes. He was adamant that if Katie and I were to be wed, we would take this property and build...well, build this. Or that I would, anyway." He ran his hand over the smooth white of the adobe walls, his eyes soft.

"You built this?" Hank stood and looked at the building. "By yourself?"

His father laughed as he paced the porch. "No, not exactly. Your mother and I did. She was very talented—much more than just in the kitchen. We got married, moved up here and started building. It was quite a task and we had a very short time to do it. We lived with her parents for a bit, then moved in as soon as we could. Didn't even have windows yet at the time, but she didn't mind. We didn't mind."

"It's a lovely place," Clara said, her heart tugging at Mr. Archer's sadness.

"Yes. We spent many, many hours on this porch, watching the sunsets. Nothing like an Arizona sunset."

He took a deep breath and continued. "When I'd left the cattle drive, my employer gave me a few head to start with on my own, and we did that up here, too. Ended up making some money and doing pretty well. Seems I had a knack for cattle driving. Just like you."

"Pa..."

"Let me finish, Hank. This is hard enough as it is," he, rubbing his eyes. "We'd been here a little while and were doing pretty well. Overjoyed to find out that your mother was with child."

"Oh, that would be me, wouldn't it?"

"Yes, yes it would, son." Hank frowned, and gazed down at the buildings of Tombstone. "Your mother had a difficult time of it, and I decided that I didn't feel comfortable with her being this far away from civilization, beautiful as it is. I'd saved some money and was able to buy the property the ranch sits on now from somebody eager to leave town to try his hand in the gold rush in California. It was a lucky day for me."

"So you moved down to the ranch?" Hank said, his eyes on his father.

"Not right away. Wasn't a stick of a building on it at the time. Your mother took you to stay with her folks for a bit, and I gathered all the help I could and built a duplicate of this very building on the ranch. It's where we lived until we built the big house we're in now."

"Oh," Clara said. "That's the white building between the house and the barn, isn't it?"

"Yes, it is."

"And that was Mama's favorite place to be. She taught the girls to paint there, read us all books there, did her sewing. It was...her place. Her garden." Hank rubbed his forehead before he sat down again on the porch swing.

"Yes. I closed it up and locked it when she passed. Haven't been in there since."

"So, I still don't understand what this has to do with my getting this property. What is so urgent about it?" Hank asked.

"If I may intrude, I think I know," Clara said. "Katie's father didn't deed you the property, obviously. You thought he had?"

"Yes, young lady. Exactly that. I'd thought it was a gift, and when he died and I heard he'd willed it to Hank—who was the only grandchild he met before he left for Colorado—I set out to keep it in the family. Couldn't bear to part with it."

"So, requiring me to be married to inherit the property—why would he have done that?"

"Oh, the old coot was a hopeless romantic. Wanted everybody to be happy, and in love. Shortly after you were born, your grandma died. Abe was heartbroken, and set out for Colorado to relieve the pain, erase some of the memories. Said he didn't want to stick around here anymore."

"Oh, my," Clara said, standing and crossing to Hank as he sat on the porch swing. "So this was sort of a ploy to ensure that his grandson was married? And hopefully happy?"

Clara's heart fluttered as she looked at Hank. She felt the warmth of his hand as he gripped hers and she realized they were sitting together on the porch swing. Beau and Katie's porch swing.

"Exactly, my dear. And that is where you come in."

Chapter Twelve

Clara and Hank rode back to the ranch in silence without even eating the picnic lunch that the housekeeper had prepared. It didn't feel appropriate to Clara to stay after all they'd heard from Beau, his emotions so close to the surface.

He'd headed out before they did and they lingered just a bit before Hank untied the wagon and helped her in.

"You didn't know any of that, Hank?" Clara asked softly as he walked around the back of the buggy. He pulled himself in and grabbed the reins.

"No, I didn't," he said, staring straight ahead, his face stony.

"Are you upset?"

His hands were tight on the reins, his knuckles almost white as he guided the horses back down the hill, the same way they'd come.

"I don't know if upset is the right word, Clara."

He glanced at her quickly and then looked ahead.

"Then what is the right word?"

"I guess I'm still a little confused," he said as he turned and looked back at the boulders where the little white house sat.

"It seems fairly straightforward. He wants to keep the property—and the house—in his family for sentimental reasons. Don't you think?" Clara pulled the picture book out from under her seat and flipped the pages, trying to locate a particular type of cactus that they were nearing as they reached the bottom of the hill. She loosened the ties of her bonnet as the heat of the valley warmed her.

"I suppose. But still, if there's a bit more time, what's the rush? Something doesn't quite add up."

"He did ask once again if we could speed things up just now. Have a wedding as soon as possible, before you left. Sounds like he really wants this."

"That's another thing I don't understand. He said himself that after he and Ma got married, he got off the trail right away. Didn't want to leave her. How could he expect any different from me? Get married and leave my wife, all in the same week?"

Clara's grip tightened on the book as she looked over at Hank. She'd not gotten any indication from him that he had thoughts that this would be a real marriage. Hope had glimmered in her several times, but she'd not seen anything from him other than a desire to be respectful and kind.

"I've resigned myself to the necessity of the marriage and all, but—"

Her head snapped forward, her heart clenching at the word, "necessity." She'd been foolish to allow herself even that faint spot of hope.

As Hank steered the wagon around a bend in the road, a sound Clara had never heard before pierced the air. The closest thing she could liken it to was the sound of a baby's rattle. But why would there be one of those here?

Both horses reared their heads and took off running, so suddenly that by the time Hank yelled, "Hold on," it was too late, and she'd fallen into the back of the buggy, knocking her head on the side.

It was but a moment before Hank had the horses slowed, then stopped, and jumped out and held each horse's bridle, talking to them soft and low until their quivers stopped, and their hooves rested rather than stomped.

In what seemed like a matter of seconds, the whole thing was over.

When the horses were still, Hank rushed around to the side of the buggy, a concerned, "Are you all right?" the first thing out of his mouth.

As her heart slowed to a regular pace, she took stock, wiggling her fingers and her toes before she realized that her skirt was up around her knees from when she'd fallen backwards.

Hank quickly turned around as he blushed, and Clara quickly pulled her skirts down where they belonged.

"I think you have a little mark on your forehead. Can I take a look?"

She reached up and felt a little dampness, pulling her hand away and flinching at the blood on it. "Yes, certainly. I'm fine," she said as she reached for her bonnet that had fallen off during the ordeal.

He reached in the buggy, holding onto her arm and helping her stand up to climb over onto the seat again. She was still in a bit of a daze as to what happened, and as he got into the buggy and took his handkerchief and dabbed the blood away, their eyes met and they both burst into laughter.

"I don't know why we're laughing. That was pretty dangerous. Rattlers can spook horses so badly that they don't stop running until they're tired."

"I think I'm laughing because nobody got hurt—not really—and that's the second time I've had to have you rescue me from a fall."

"I don't think this one counts. I caused the fall," he said, frowning as he looked back. "Or the rattler did, I should say."

"Is that what that was? A rattlesnake?" She shivered as she had the first time she'd seen a picture of one in her book.

"It was. Didn't get a good look as I was trying to hold the horses, but from the sound, I'd say it was good-sized."

"You sure calmed the horses down quickly," she said, thinking of how he'd spoken to them softly and they'd just…stopped.

"Ah. Yes, these are two of my horses. Two that

I've trained. They know me."

She recognized Major, now that he'd mentioned it. "I've watched you with the horses, Hank. They seem to...listen to you."

The reins clicked as he hurried the horses along. "I don't know about that. And don't mention that to Pa. He thinks it's a bunch of hogwash. But I do sometimes feel like I...hear them. Know what they're thinking."

Clara fell silent, thinking of the horses in Chicago. She'd felt the same thing. She just knew they were cold, uncomfortable and needed help. Like Hank, she didn't know *how* she knew. She just knew.

And now, thinking of Beau and his story about his wife, his need for this property, she felt she knew what she needed to do.

"Hank, as this is a marriage of convenience, to enable you to inherit the property, where would I be staying after? I mean, you know, when we're..."

"Married?" he said.. "I don't rightly know. I hadn't thought about it. I'm sorry. Everything happened so fast."

"You don't have a home of your own and it

wouldn't be appropriate for us to stay…well, completely together." The color crept into her cheeks even as she willed it not to. She knew she'd come to get married, so this shouldn't be a surprise.

"I'd ask Pa if we could stay in the casita—that's what we called Ma's little house—since it has a separate bedroom, but somehow, I don't think he'd be amenable." Hank shook his head, the frustration apparent as he gripped the reins more tightly.

"I suppose I could just stay in the big house. It's huge, even with all the girls. I think on our tour I spotted an empty bedroom."

Hank turned to her, frowning. "I don't know what I *did* have in mind, Clara, but that wasn't it." He turned back toward the road as they drew closer to the ranch. "Besides, it's not urgent. We have time to come up with a plan."

Clara smiled and placed her hand on Hank's forearm. "No, we don't have time. If it's all right with you, I'd like to go ahead with the wedding. As soon as possible. I'd like your father to have what he wants. That is what I came here for, after all."

Hank pulled the horses to a stop, turning to Clara. "Are you sure, Clara? There's no emergency. I want you to be satisfied that you'll at least be welcome and—hopefully—content. I can't offer much more than that right now."

Clara looked down at her hands clasped around the book. She picked it up and held it to her chest as she turned to Hank.

"I'm sure. I came for a new, happy life and I mean to have one."

Hank's blue eyes twinkled as he leaned forward, then caught himself, sitting upright again as he cleared his throat. He pulled his hat down further on his forehead and flicked the reins.

"Thank you, Clara. I'm mighty grateful, and Pa will be, too."

Clara's heart slowed to normal after it had taken off like the horses when Hank had leaned in toward her. Had she wanted him to kiss her? The foolishness of that thought struck her like lightning. This was a marriage in name only, and she'd best keep all other thoughts out of her head.

Chapter Thirteen

Everything had moved so quickly, Clara wasn't sure which way was up. She couldn't forget sensing Beau's relief as she and Hank told him of their decision. They did both chuckle when, after he'd regained his composure, he'd asked, "How about tomorrow?"

"Tomorrow?" Clara had said, her body stiffening for a moment before she relaxed into the decision again, knowing she was doing the right thing.

Hank's anxious frown smoothed away as she said, "Tomorrow would be fine if we can get a license and pastor in time. I don't know how long it takes—"

Beau held up his index finger as he turned and reached into a roll-top desk and pulled out a piece of paper, handing it to Hank.

"You went ahead and applied for a marriage

license for us?"

Beau put his thumbs in the sides of his black, satin vest as his chest puffed out. He rocked forward and backward on his leather boots. "I did. Thought it would save time when you two did decide, and the courthouse said all you need to do is sign it and add the date. And Pastor Grayson's been on alert, too."

Clara let out a breath as she took a peek at the marriage license with her name on it, and she struggled to take a breath back in as it all suddenly became very real.

Her eyes met Hank's, and he folded the paper and handed it back to Beau. "You okay with tomorrow, Clara?"

Her hands went to her earrings—the pearls from her mother—and she stood tall, saying, "Yes. Yes, I'm sure, and tomorrow is fine."

Her own personal butterflies that resided in her stomach—as she now thought of them—took flight as Hank smiled at her, his laugh lines etched in his tanned, handsome face. He took her hand, his eyes twinkling as he kissed the back of it and quietly said, "Thank you."

"Oh, yes, thank you," Beau said, almost as an afterthought as he replaced the marriage license back in the desk and rolled the top shut.

"I presume that James and Suzanne can bring you tomorrow. We'll have the wedding here, and maybe lunch at the Occidental if I can arrange it. Noon would be fine.." Beau's voice trailed off as he headed into the kitchen—to make the arrangements for her wedding, she presumed.

As soon as he was out of earshot, they both laughed, Clara putting her hand over her mouth so as not to be overheard.

"Well, looks like this is it," Hank said, pacing the floor in long strides, his hands behind him.

She reached out and stopped him, looking up at him as he turned to her. "Don't worry, Hank. It'll be fine. I never thought much about what kind of wedding I'd have, only the kind of marriage it would be."

"Oh," he said, his hands clasped behind him. "I do promise to keep you safe, and try my darndest to make you happy, Clara. That, I can promise."

Her heart pinched at the sincerity in his voice, and once again, she'd felt she was making the right decision. As she'd glanced around her future home with new eyes, she hoped this wouldn't be the first time her instincts failed her.

Now, after another night of tossing and turning in her bed, she was less certain. She had hung up all of her dresses when she'd arrived, but they were all too wrinkled—and too warm—to get married in. She put on a day dress, wondering how much time she had to pull something together.

At least that was all she had to worry about. She'd talked with Sadie and Suzanne when she got home—between shrieks and laughter—and they'd settled on the wedding at Archer Ranch and a small luncheon at the Occidental afterward. There were no guests other than family to be invited, so the group would be small enough to be in the small dining room to the side of the restaurant, with long, red velvet curtains to close for privacy.

She wrung her hands as she looked once more in her wardrobe. Suzanne had offered the dress she and Sadie had both married in, and it did look like it would fit—and was lovely. For some reason, though she'd wanted something of her own. Why hadn't she thought to bring something more appropriate from Chicago?

She jumped at the knock on her door as it pulled her away from her thoughts. "Come in," she said as she moved to open the door.

Backing away as it opened to allow enough room for the twins and Suzanne to enter, she looked with surprise to Suzanne. The twins struggled with each end of a rather large, flat box, and Suzanne shrugged as they finally made it to the bed and set it down.

"This just came for you. I think I recognized the deliverer from Archer Ranch, but I'm not positive. There's a note."

"Hurry up and open it, Clara!" Lucy cried, sitting on the bed beside her and bouncing up and down.

"Is it candy?" Lily said as she stood beside Clara, her eyes wide.

"I don't think so," Suzanne said as she moved to sit at the vanity.

Clara held the note in her hand, the gold-embossed

'A' in the left corner letting her know it was from the Archer Ranch.

"Do you think it could be a wedding gift from Hank? How thoughtful," Clara said as she turned the envelope over and opened it.

She read the letter silently and looked up as it dropped to her lap. She frowned at Suzanne, and set it to the side, picking up the box and untying the ribbon that surrounded it.

"Well, what did it say? What is it?" Suzanne said as she stood and moved closer for a better look.

"Just one line. From Mr. Archer." Clara removed the ribbon, wrapping it around Lucy's neck as she giggled. "It just says that he wants me to have this to wear today. It was Katie's."

Suzanne gasped as Clara took the lid off the box and lifted up a beautiful, sky blue chiffon dress.

Clara blinked hard as she looked at it, her eyes moist as she looked from the dress to Suzanne.

"It's beautiful, Aunt Clara," Lily said.

Lucy reached out to touch the soft chiffon. "You'll look like a princess again."

"Stay right here. We have just the thing, don't

we girls?" Suzanne said over her shoulder as she left, both twins in tow.

Clara walked slowly to the mirror, holding the dress in front of her. The color was stunning, and she spun in a circle, laughing at the way the chiffon followed her with a flounce.

As she regarded herself one more time, wondering if it would be appropriate to wear it for the wedding, Suzanne held up a pair of ice blue earrings, the exact color of the dress, and placed a hat on her head.

"Look at how beautiful this color is with your red hair and green eyes," Suzanne said softly. "And it's warm now that it's spring. The hat will do you well."

Clara reached for the earrings and held it to her ear. She hadn't given much thought to her actual wedding, really, and was pleased with what she saw. She hoped Hank would be, too.

"You think I should wear it, then?" She turned to Suzanne who regarded her with her arms folded.

"I think there is absolutely no question that you should."

Clara turned back to the mirror and frowned, holding the shoulders of the dress where they would rest—a bit off her shoulders. "You don't think it immodest with my shoulders exposed?"

"Certainly not. Katie Archer was well loved and well respected. If it was good enough for her, it's fine for you, too." She walked behind Clara, taking the shoulders and holding them to Clara, peeking around her into the mirror.

"You have to wear it. You have to," Lily said as she peered into the mirror from behind Clara's skirts.

Clara smiled down at the twins. Her eyes met Suzanne's in the mirror and she nodded. "I will. It will be an honor."

"Good, that's settled. I'll go heat some water so you can have a bath, and make you something for breakfast." Suzanne carefully laid the dress on the bed. "You're sure you don't need to wear your mother's earrings? For courage?"

Clara picked up the hem of the beautiful dress, rubbing the soft chiffon between her fingers. "No, I don't believe so. I don't feel fearful. Not one bit," she said as she followed Suzanne out the door.

Chapter Fourteen

Hank and the rest of the guests were already on the back patio of the ranch when Clara arrived, James at the reins of the buggy. Her heart thudded in her chest as she gripped the small bouquet of flowers the twins had given her before they'd left for Archer Ranch with their mother, Tripp and Sadie.

She shifted from foot to foot, smoothing her dress, for what seemed like ages before James came back out and said, "They're ready."

He smiled as he offered her his arm, having said he was honored to be chosen to walk her down the aisle. She squeezed as she put her arm through his, looking into his kind eyes as she remembered their time in Chicago while he courted Suzanne.

A lilting melody drifted through the open door as Hank's six sisters began to sing, and James gently led Clara through the house to the patio.

Her friends and future family stood to each side of the patio stuffed with flowers of all kinds, some in pots and some in vases, and it took her a moment to look up and notice Hank, his shock apparent as he looked at the dress she was wearing. Concern flitted through her head that she'd made the wrong decision, worried that he was upset, but she breathed a sigh of relief as he smiled, meeting her eyes as he took her hand from James.

The pastor spoke quickly, Clara lost in her thoughts as she looked from the pastor to Hank and back to the pastor. She hadn't even thought about this part, so when she was prompted to say, "I do," she did. Plain and simple.

As the pastor pronounced them man and wife, her butterflies returned when Hank leaned toward her, hesitated, and leaned further in, his warm lips brushing hers. Six titters—no, eight if you counted the twins—broke the spell as he moved away and reddened. He turned, a mock scowl aimed at his sisters, who immediately looked at the floor and fell silent, although unable to wipe the grins off their faces.

"Congratulations to the newlyweds," her new

father-in-law was the first to say as Clara and Hank turned to shake hands and receive hugs while Beau reached into his pocket for the marriage license and a pen.

"Could you please come with me for a moment?" he said quietly as he guided Clara by her elbow into the house and spread the license out on the table, handing her the pen and an inkpot to dip it in.

"Pa, right now?" Hank said as he followed them inside.

"Yes, now. Then we can go right to the Occidental." He smiled and nodded at Clara as she dipped the quill and signed her name in the spot he had indicated. She handed the pen to Hank, who did the same and thrust the pen toward his father and pulled Clara back out onto the patio.

"I'll lead the way in case you all don't know where the Occidental is," Tripp said as everyone laughed and headed toward their buggies.

Clara pondered what Hank had thought about his father on the short ride to the restaurant. He'd explained yesterday that it was to keep the property in the family. If she recalled correctly, she'd heard when she first arrived that if Hank had not been married when the appropriate time period ran out the property would be donated to…something. Somewhere. She reached back in to her memory but couldn't grab the name. Everything had been so new, and things had moved so fast.

"I still think it's for sentimental reasons," Clara said as they walked into the small dining room at the restaurant to applause and stopped short as her eyes fell on the most beautiful wedding cake she'd ever seen, its white frosting dotted with rose petals. She turned to search for Sadie, rushing to hug her friend.

"However did you do this so quickly?" Her eyes took in the buffet of wonderful food that had been prepared in their honor.

"I have no doubt that you can remember how early we bakers rise when need be," Sadie said. "It's in our blood—and even easier to do for such a happy occasion." She squeezed her hand as she whispered in her ear, "Congratulations, my friend. I know you will be very happy."

Clara glanced quickly at Hank, hoping that her friend was right.

"This was so kind of you to do," Hank said to Sadie as he stood by Clara's side, his smile genuine.

"Think nothing of it," Tripp said. "I did invite someone, though, so I hope you don't mind." He looked past Hank over his shoulder and waved.

Clara and Hank both turned, Hank extending his hand as he clapped his friend on the back. "Clara, please meet my old friend, Samuel Ford. I didn't get a chance to introduce you when we were here for dinner the other night."

Samuel bowed slightly toward Clara. "You must be the most beautiful bride I've ever seen, ma'am. Hank, you're a lucky man." He stood and looked around the room, winking at Tripp and James. "You're all mighty lucky to have found such good women."

The twins laughed and Clara reddened.

"Don't listen to him, Clara. He's a charmer, that one. That's how he does so well behind the bar."

Samuel clapped his hand on Hank's back. "I never tell a lie, Suzanne. You've known me a long time. I just say what I mean and mean what I say."

"And that's why we thought you'd be perfect

behind the bar, Samuel. Thanks for joining us," Tripp said, shaking the hand of the tall, thin man with laughing green eyes.

"It's an honor," Samuel said as he moved into the corner where her father-in-law stood, watching the event unfold. As Samuel approached, they fell deep into conversation, their heads together as they spoke quietly.

Hank steered Clara over to the cake by her elbow, whispering, "Do we need to go to Suzanne's to get your things?"

"No, I packed this morning before we left. Everything is ready. James unloaded my bags onto the porch before we left the house."

"Oh, good," he said as he handed Clara the knife to cut the cake. "I have an appointment this afternoon at the barn that I can't miss."

Startled, she said, "Today? On our wedding day?"

He took a step back. "I didn't know today would be our wedding day until last night. I couldn't change it, and it's very important. I'm sure you understand."

Sadie had plated several pieces of cake and

handed one of the rich, dark chocolate confections to Clara. "Pay attention, everybody. It's time for the bride and groom to have the first piece of cake."

"Of course, I understand." She smiled at her friends and new family, turned to Hank and smeared the chocolate cake right on his face.

Chapter Fifteen

Hank had eyed her warily after the cake incident, but seemed not to be bothered after he'd been given a napkin and cleaned up. Mercifully, he hadn't done the same to her.

They'd been the first to leave due to Hank's appointment, and he'd said he wanted to see her settled in her new room before the arrival of whomever he expected.

Hank pulled the buggy up to the front of the ranch house and went around, helping her out. He didn't release her hand right away, and took his hat off, and said, "You look beautiful, Clara, and thank you for wearing my mother's dress."

She looked down, smoothing her skirts. "I notice that the tie you're wearing matches," she said, referring to the turquoise bolo tie he had on, the light blue color the exact shade as the dress.

"My father gave it to me right before the

wedding. I didn't know why, but I wore it out of respect. My guess would be it's what he wore when they got married."

"Did you know your father had sent the dress?" She pulled her hand away and started up the steps to the house. Hank pulled his hat down and followed.

"No, he hadn't told me. I still think there's something strange going on."

Clara waited as Hank opened the door for her, ushering her inside. "If you'll follow me, I'll show you to your room. I hope you don't mind joining in with the crowd in the house, but there's not a choice for now. Besides, when I head out on the trail next week, it'll be better for you to have company."

She followed him down a long hallway with doors on both the left and the right, and into the one she'd seen during their brief tour before.

Hank set her bags down on the small, wooden bench at the foot of the bed as she looked around. The room was cool due to the thick adobe walls, the window open to the garden behind the house.

The doors to the large, dark wood wardrobe

stood open, its shelves empty. Hank followed her gaze and said, "The room is all ready for you. Our housekeeper will be in shortly to help you unpack."

She turned from the window and walked toward the bed. "That won't be necessary, really. You go on ahead to your appointment. I can manage."

Hank sighed and looked back out the door to the grandfather clock that stood in the hall. "I really do have to go, Clara. I'll be back later this evening for supper. And please do take advantage of Maria, at least to show you around to the facilities."

Clara took off her white gloves and laid them down with her hat on the bed. "Really, Hank, I'll be fine. Please, go ahead." She smiled weakly as he hesitated then left, shutting the door behind him.

"Some wedding day," she muttered, propping her head on the windowsill and dropping her chin into her hands. She shook her head, trying to rid herself of the thoughts that clamored in. It really had been a beautiful wedding, her friends going to a great deal of trouble—particularly with the short notice. She reminded herself to be more grateful.

Clara banged her head on the top of the short window frame as a, "Hello," jarred her out of her self-pity.

Rubbing the top of her head, she peered out the window, greeted by the shy face of Saffron, one of the twins. The longest, most beautiful eyelashes Clara had ever seen fluttered over big, brown eyes, her shy smile welcome.

"Hello to you, too," Clara said, accepting the single daisy that Saffron held out to her.

"I wasn't sure that we needed any more sisters at first, but Pepper said we didn't have a choice, that it's what Papa wanted."

Clara groaned, once again reminded of her place—and purpose—in this household. "Thank you for the flower, Saffron. I will try to be a good sister, as all of your others are."

Saffron laughed, her hand to her mouth. "Who said they're good sisters? Not all the time, anyway."

"Oh," Clara said as she laughed, thinking of Lucy and Lily. "Hopefully, I'll be one of the good ones. I'd like to be, anyway."

"I hope so, too." Saffron walked away slowly,

but stopped as Clara said, "Thank you for welcoming me to your household. I imagine it has been a bit of a surprise."

Saffron looked at her intently, walking back over and squeezing her hand through the window, to Clara's surprise. "We've had some time to get used to it. I, for one, am glad you're here." Her shy smile returned before she ran off further into the garden.

Clara pulled her head back in the window. Holding the daisy to her cheek, her heart filled with warmth at the shy greeting she'd just received.

She moved to the door when a soft rap came, thinking it was the housekeeper to help her get settled. "Thank you very much but I don't need—"

She stopped mid-sentence at the sight of her new father-in-law outside of her door. He looked down at his polished boots, his hands clasped behind his back, his head popping up as she opened the door.

"Hello, Clara. I didn't mean to startle you. I just wanted to thank you for today. I'm sure you know how much it means to me," he said.

"I do, Mr. Archer. And thank you for the dress. It was an honor to wear it."

His eyes misted as he looked down at the dress Clara still wore. Clearing his throat, he said, "I'm glad that you wore it. It looks lovely on you."

She stood waiting as he looked around. "Where is Hank?"

Clara sighed. "We had to come back early. He said he had an appointment, down at the barn, I believe."

His lips fell in a thin line. "Is he messing around breaking horses again?" He looked out the window in the direction of the barn.

"I don't know, exactly, but I think so. Isn't that what he does best?"

"Best? It depends on how you define best. Hank is the best trail boss I've ever seen. And he's heading out in a few days, so he should be getting ready for that, not training some stranger's horses."

Clara watched as her father-in-law grew more agitated with every word. She squared her shoulders, and even though she was angry with Hank, she said, "Mr. Archer, shouldn't people be able to choose what they *want* to be best at? He's awfully good with horses. They listen to him."

"Listen to him?" he scoffed. "Don't be silly. Horses don't 'listen', they only know what they're told to do."

She lifted her chin and continued. "I've seen him with the horses and it's...special."

Beau fumed in front of her, his hands clenching. "Now, young lady, we have a business to run, and it has priorities. There's no time for him to chase those fantasies of his that the horses 'listen' to him. There are cattle to be run."

"I'm sorry. I was just trying to say—"

"I know what you were trying to say, and I'll have none of it. And truthfully, it's not any of your business. Now, if you'll excuse me..." he said as he gave her a curt nod and turned on his heel toward the front door.

Clara shut the door and plopped on the bed. She worried the hem of her dress and reached into her valise to find another one, more suitable. Or at least durable.

As she hung the crystal blue wedding dress in the wardrobe, she smoothed it, tucking it in, wondering how she would ever fit here. Clearly, she'd been told to mind her own business. She wasn't sure that was something she could do now that she knew her husband needed her.

Chapter Sixteen

She decided to head down to the barn to see Hank after she'd finished putting her clothes away. Maria, the housekeeper, had come by to check on her, and they'd made an arrangement for a tour later in the evening.

Clara strolled down the long drive, slowing as she passed the small, white house with the blue window frames. She stopped in front of the small iron gate that led into a patio area filled with the neglected shrubs and herb plants she'd noticed before. Several bright scarlet flowers struggled to break through a tangle of weeds and she looked left and right before she opened the gate and went in.

She bent down and quickly cleared away the weeds so that the plants might have half a chance to break through and produce even more blooms. Looking around and seeing no one, she put her nose to the window to see what was inside, and was met with flowered fabric covering the glass on the inside.

"Darn," she muttered under her breath as she turned and went back out the gate, pulling it shut behind her. Now that she knew this had been Katie's special house, and that Mr. Archer had closed it up after she died, she was even more curious to peek inside.

The sputters and neighs of horses neighing carried through the door as she approached the barn. She slowed again, wondering which part of the barn Hank was in. She opened her mouth to call out to him just as she approached and stopped as she noticed the barn door was open. Something made her slow even more and poked her head around the corner.

The ten stalls she'd noticed the day before each held a horse, beautiful ones of all colors and types. She'd seen some of them in the book she'd brought and recognized a palomino and what she thought might be a quarter horse, but she wasn't sure. Some smaller horses, younger, she guessed, were in stalls with larger horses.

The barn was empty—of humans, anyway—so she entered, expecting to see Hank maybe in the arena. As she walked through, she gravitated to the left side, petting the noses of all the horses she passed as they eagerly thrust their heads out, neighing slightly as she touched them.

As she approached the open door at the opposite end of the barn, she turned around, each horse now on the right side of the barn looking at her intently. On the left, the horses stomped and whinnied, some of them even kicking their doors as she passed. She shook her head as she remembered what Hank had said about the horses he'd broken being on one side and other horses—maybe trail horses—on the other. There was no question in her mind which side held the horses Hank had trained.

She turned again and walked toward the shade covering the benches beside the arena, pulling her bonnet down to shade her eyes from the piercing sunlight.

Hank looked up at her and smiled as he held the lead of a smaller horse, a beautiful white one, as it circled around him. She'd never seen anything like this before, and wondered if they were just having fun or if there was some purpose to what he was doing.

She reached the benches and sat down beside a young couple, with a young girl who looked to be six or seven sitting on the young woman's lap.

"Hello," she said to the woman as she sat on the bench next to her under the shade of the towering tree, nodding toward the young family.

"Oh, hello," the woman said, sitting the young girl down on the bench between the young man and her. "Would you be Hank's new wife?" She extended her hand to Clara as she felt heat creep into her cheeks. His wife?

She cleared her throat, willing her flushed cheeks to cool. "Well, yes, I suppose I am," she said, shaking the woman's hand. "My name's Clara Martin...er, Clara Archer."

The woman wrapped both of her hands around Clara's. "Oh, Mrs. Archer, I'm so terribly sorry that we've interrupted your wedding day. Hank told us when we got here. Thank you for accommodating our final training. Today is the day we get to pick up Abigail's horse, and we wanted to make sure he was safe for Abigail to ride. And Hank's the only one we trust around here for that. The only one Frank and I felt comfortable with." She gestured toward the bench as she looked toward Hank, her hand over her eyes as she squinted in his direction.

"Please don't worry, Mrs. Beckett. Hank takes this very seriously, and I don't believe he would have cancelled for anything in the world." *Including me.*

The woman wrung her hands. "Well, I do apologize, though. If we weren't riding to Tucson tomorrow, we would have left as soon as we heard."

Clara smiled as she watched Hank in the hot sun, patiently running the young horse through its paces, seemingly pleased with what he saw.

"Can you believe he does all this without even using a whip? Amazing that he can train like this just using his voice." Mrs. Beckett shook her head slowly, watching Hank with gleaming admiration.

"People use whips? On horses?" Clara's hand moved to her chest, her mouth open.

Mrs. Beckett broke her gaze away from Hank's progress and turned to Clara. "It's not quite like it sounds. It's the way horses are broken, normally, and in the right hands, it's guidance rather than painful punishment. But Hank, somehow, doesn't even need one. Just his voice..." She trailed off, looking back to her daughter as she and her father watched Hank intently.

"Hmph," muttered a voice behind them.

They both turned at the sound, Mrs. Beckett smiling and walking over, her hand extended.

"Hello, Mr. Archer."

Good day, Mrs. Beckett."

"Isn't it remarkable what your son does with these horses?"

Mr. Archer repeated his previous comment as Clara pulled the brim of her bonnet down further and smiled.

"What is it, Mr. Archer? Surely, you must be aware what a gift he has. And what a gift he is to those of us who want gentle, safe horses in our stables." She turned and winked at Clara before walking back to her family and sitting on the bench.

Her father-in-law folded his arms over his chest as he glared at his son in the center of the arena. Shaking his head, he turned on his heel and walked into the barn.

Clara moved over to where Mrs. Beckett

watched Hank and sat beside her.

Mrs. Beckett eyed Clara. "Don't worry, Mrs. Archer. It will get better. This has been a long-standing issue between Hank and his father. I'm sure it'll be settled sometime. We've known the Archer family a long time, and things are...difficult now. I believe Mr. Archer will see that Hank is much more valuable here, training horses, than out on the trail."

They continued to watch as Hank wiped his brow with his handkerchief, leading the horse out the gate of the arena. He walked into the barn, and Clara and the young family followed.

As they entered the barn, Hank placed the riding blanket on the horse, and then the saddle, cinching it tightly before he placed the bridle over its head and the bit in its mouth. The horse objected for a moment, and Hank bent down, whispering in its ear, and Clara's eyes widened as the mare immediately settled.

Hank winked at Abigail and said, "You ready for a ride? I need to teach you a few things before you go. Teach you how to talk to him, too."

Abigail laughed as Hank lifted her on the horse,

her hands immediately going to the saddle horn. "I see you've done this once or twice," he said, smiling at Abigail as he led the horse back out into the arena.

Mrs. Beckett sighed, the look of gratitude unmistakable as she watched her daughter and her new horse enter the arena.

Clara's new insight into what Hank wanted to do—no, needed to do—made her wonder exactly what his father was so opposed to. And she was fairly certain it was going to get worse before it got better.

Chapter Seventeen

The day had been very long, and Clara retreated to her room after the riding lesson, not sure where else to go. When Maria knocked on her door and told her that supper was ready, she sighed, preparing herself for anything.

She was pleasantly surprised that the food was excellent—although she'd never heard of, let alone eaten, enchiladas before—and as the easy conversation slowed, Clara stood from the table, the unusual meal that Maria had provided still tingling on her tongue.

"That was delicious, and like nothing I've ever tasted before."

Maria's thick, black braid swung as she turned around and motioned for Clara to sit.

"Was it too hot for you, Señora?" she asked as she wiggled her finger at Sage and Saffron, whose job it apparently was to clear the dishes after supper. "Come now, ladies. I am a housekeeper, not a maid."

"Hot?" Clara asked, a quizzical glance at Hank as she took her seat.

"Maria's from Mexico, and we've grown accustomed to food the way it's prepared there," Mr. Archer said, leaning back in his chair and steepling his fingers. "Not many people can handle it."

"Oh, Mr. Beau, I made it special for Miss Clara. Not too spicy. Was it okay?" She eagerly turned to Clara as the girls took the dishes into the kitchen.

"Absolutely wonderful," Clara said, lifting her water glass and nodding in appreciation.

Maria's smile spread wide as she nodded in return, wiping her hands on her apron as she turned to go back into the kitchen as well.

"Pa, may we be excused?" Pepper, the youngest of Hank's sisters asked.

Beau turned to his daughter, his eyes soft.

"I don't know. Let's ask the question, shall we?"

Pepper groaned, turning to her sisters and saying, "Has everyone finished with their chores?"

"Papa, you know we always finish before supper." Pepper laughed as she looked around at her sisters, nodding.

He smiled warmly as he looked around the table.

"Thank you very much. You may be excused."

"Oh, one thing," Clara said as they pushed their chairs back from the table. "I wanted to thank you all for welcoming me into your home. And for your lovely song today. It made the wedding special."

They looked to their father before casting their eyes around, most of them ultimately settling on their feet.

He gave a curt nod as he looked at his daughter, tacit permission for them to leave, and they did—all together and in quite a rush.

"You don't have to tell them twice," Hank said as the last of his sisters pulled the door closed behind them.

"Hank, would you step outside with me for a moment? On the porch? I have some things to discuss with you."

"Sure, Pa, let me just get Clara a wrap and we'll

be—"

"Just you, son," Beau said over his shoulder as he walked toward the porch.

He stopped with his hand on the doorknob and turned to Clara, his gaze stern.

"You don't mind, do you? Family business."

Clara's breath caught in her throat at the unmistakable message. She wasn't family.

"Pa, we just got married today, and I was hoping to spend some time with my—"

Clara wrapped her arms around herself, backing up slowly toward the kitchen. "It's fine, Hank. I'll go help in the kitchen."

Hank threw up his hands. He shrugged at Clara as he scowled at his father's back and followed him out the door.

"I won't be long, Clara. We'll sit out?"

"That would be nice, Hank, but I truly don't want to intrude."

Hank let out a heavy sigh and shook his head as he closed the door behind him.

Clara pushed the door open into the kitchen,

pausing as she heard Sage say, "Pa says it's only for a little while. She's just here until he gets the property, and then that's it."

"I guess there's really no point in getting to know her," Saffron said. "She sure seems nice, though. She liked the flower I gave her."

"You gave her a flower? Don't do things like that. If you like her, it'll be harder when she leaves. Just like Mama."

Metal clattered and Clara jumped as Maria said, "Girls. You cannot be like your father, afraid to be hurt. That is no way to live. You won't feel pain, but you also won't feel joy. It isn't right."

"But Maria, Papa wasn't like this before Mama died. He says not to let yourself get hurt like that. Like he did."

"I don't care what he says. And you can tell him I said that. He is not himself."

"Well, I'm going to do what he says, anyway," Saffron said. "He knows best."

"You always do what he says," her sister said. "That's why you're no fun."

The swinging door pushed Clara back against

the wall as Saffron ran out, laughing as Sage chased her. "I'll show you who's no fun."

Clara pressed her hand against her heart, willing it to stop beating so quickly.

"Hey, you two, slow down," Maria shouted as she walked out of the kitchen. She gathered another stack of dishes and gasped as she turned and saw Clara, her face beet red and her eyes downcast.

"Oh, Miss Clara. I didn't know you were here." Maria sat down at the table, patting the chair next to her.

Clara took a deep breath, her pride stung as she slowly reached the table and sat beside Maria.

"Is it true? Mr. Archer thinks I'm not staying? He wants me to leave?"

Maria shook her head slowly, taking Clara's hand and squeezing. "I'm sorry you heard that, Miss Clara. The girls—well, since their mother died, it's been very difficult here. So many hurt people. No one really talking. So they get things in their heads and I don't know where it comes from."

Clara's eyes misted as she felt the lingering

sadness tug her heart again.

"You feel it, don't you? I knew you did."

"I wasn't sure what I felt, but I do believe that's it. Lots of grief here." She pulled her handkerchief from her sleeve and ran it over her brow. "I can see it in their eyes."

Maria's eyes sparkled. "Yes, I can see that. And you know what else I see?"

Clara looked up at Maria, surprised to see her smiling.

"I see the way Mr. Hank looks at you. It has been a few short days, but I also see how Miss Saffron looks at you. You have brought more life into this house in those days than has been here in a year."

Clara's hands tingled and she laughed.

"And I see how you look at him, too," Maria said quietly, her kind smile giving Clara some comfort.

"None of that matters, Maria, if Mr. Archer wants me to be gone. I imagine if that's what he wants, that's what will happen. And Hank will be leaving on the trail soon..."

Maria shook her head firmly and stood, her hands on her hips.

"This has been going on long enough and he needs to stop this business of trying to control everything to protect his heart. If he doesn't stop, he'll lose Mr. Hank, and then all of you, too, will want to leave."

Clara stood, picking up some of the dishes from the table as she sighed.

"I don't know quite what to do. I want—"

"You want what?" Hank said as he came through the door, his cheeks flushed.

Clara looked quickly to Maria as Hank began to shove the chairs back under the table.

Maria winked at Clara and said, "I'll be in the kitchen if you need me. Mr. Hank, there's some lemonade on the side table out on the back patio for you two."

Chapter Eighteen

As Maria retreated into the kitchen, Hank pushed in the last chair, running his hands through his dark hair.

He took a deep breath and looked up at Clara, noticeably trying to calm down.

"Hank, are you all right?"

He turned and looked at the front door, then grabbed her hand and pulled her in the opposite direction, to the back patio.

He pulled the glass doors closed behind him, gesturing for her to sit in one of the wicker chairs. He poured a glass of lemonade, handing it to her before he sat on the bench opposite her.

She sipped her lemonade, her hands trembling. She watched as a hummingbird flitted near her, buzzing in the scarlet flower of the potted plant at the edge of the patio.

It hadn't occurred to her that this might be a

temporary situation, but overhearing the girls in the kitchen had thrown her. So much so that she didn't know what to say, remaining silent and hoping that Hank would clear this all up.

Hank rested his elbows on his knees as his head fell into his hands.

Clara's mind still reeled with what she'd heard from the girls and Maria, but she set her lemonade down and moved over beside Hank on the bench.

She rested her hand on his shoulder and waited.

Hank looked up as the hummingbird made another visit, this time to the wide open yellow flowers in the pot next to him. The buzzing of its wings snapped him out of his thoughts and he turned to Clara.

"My father has some very definite ideas about my life, and how I'm supposed to live it, I'm afraid."

"He certainly does seem to have a very set plan for his family. For his ranch."

Clara leaned back against the wall of the house, her hands folded in her lap to keep them still.

Her voice quiet, she said, "What does he want you to do, Hank? I've been wondering what part I play in this."

She wondered if he knew that Beau felt this was a temporary arrangement. Maybe they'd planned that together?

Hank stood, pacing back and forth across the patio.

"For a few years now, when I'm not on the trail I've been taking in and breaking horses as a favor. Breaking's not even a good word. I just try to get them to understand what their jobs will be."

Clara leaned forward and picked up her lemonade. She took a sip, her eyes not leaving Hank as he continued to pace.

"Some are going to pull wagons, some will be herding cattle. Heck, some will even be going to California. But somehow, I can get them to understand. And once they do, they become members of a team."

Clara cleared her throat. "I've seen how you do that. You have a way with horses, Hank. Mrs. Beckett said so herself the other day at the arena."

He stopped mid-stride as he turned to meet her

gaze. His brows tugged together as his hands went to his hips.

"What do you mean?"

"Surely, you know. You have a way with horses, and people notice. I notice. You have a calming influence, even with horses you don't know."

"Oh, don't be silly. I just enjoy working with them, and we seem to get along. It's that way with anybody, isn't it?"

Clara stood, walking along the edge of the patio. "I don't believe so. I've not been here very long, but it seems to me to be different with you. You yourself know there's a difference between the horses you've trained on one side of the stables to the other horses. They seem much more agitated."

Hank rubbed the back of his neck before turning his gaze to the horizon.

"Even if that were true—which I'm not sure it is and my father would never accept—it doesn't really matter."

"It doesn't? Don't you want to spend more time at it? Mrs. Beckett implied that there were a great many people who would love to acquire your services."

Hank sighed heavily and leaned against the post at the corner of the patio.

"You have no way of knowing this, Clara, but my father hasn't been the same since my mother passed away."

He looked down at his feet as his boots shuffled on the brick.

"He wasn't always this way."

"What way? Determined to control the decisions and destiny of those around him?"

Clara set her lemonade down on the table a little more firmly than she had intended, the loud clatter making Hank turn quickly.

"Is that what it seems like? Yes, I suppose it would. To my mind, he's just trying to keep the family business on track. Keep everything the same. Said he needs me on the trail. Nobody else is good enough to do it, he told me. Nobody he trusts, anyway."

"Is that the truth? Is there no one else who could take over that responsibility?" She sat back down on the bench and shifted in her seat as he sat beside her.

"No, of course not. Truly, I don't understand what is happening here. Before my mother died and Tripp left the trail to go to chef school, we'd all agreed that I was next. That it was time for me to come off the trail and start a life of my own."

"That sounds reasonable. Especially if you want to have a family." Heat crept to her cheeks as she looked away from him, grabbing her lemonade again for something to keep her hands steady.

"I do, Clara. I really do. But he's insisting that I go out, that it's critical to the family business. And how can I have a family of my own when I'm gone most of the year?"

The girls' words rushed through her mind as the word 'temporary' flashed before her, big and bold as if it were on the marquee of a theater.

"You know, I've had an opportunity to observe many things here in the past few days. Your father's grief at the property was impossible to miss."

"I know. Like I said, he hasn't been the same since Mama died."

She rested her hand on his arm. "Sometimes it takes people a long time to grieve a loss like that.

Sadie had great difficulty in the months after her parents died, and she worked like a demon. I think to avoid thinking about it, for one thing,"

"Yes, it's not been easy for any of us."

"And as it was with Sadie, keeping to her normal schedule, keeping everything routine, I believe comforted her. A loss like that is a big change, and it's natural for people in such pain to want everything else around them to stay the same. Almost as if any more change would be too much to bear."

Hank turned to her, his head cocked to the side and his voice steady. "Clara, I think you may have hit on something. The more I try to pull away, the more tightly he holds on. Could it be that this is why?"

"That would be my guess," she said, leaning back again and nodding her head slowly.

"I don't know how I can change it. This ranch is my life, too, and if he won't change his mind, I'll be going out on the trail, no matter what I want. And soon."

He reached to his side, picking a bright yellow flower. He turned to her as he spun the stem in his fingers.

"Thank you, Clara. I appreciate your understanding with all this. Seems you understand it a far sight better than we do."

She smiled as Hank handed her the flower, her hand brushing against his as she took it.

Hank pulled his hat further down his forehead and cleared his throat. "I don't see any way to change things right now, Clara, but believe me when I say I'll come up with something. Somehow."

Taking a deep breath, she decided to assume that Hank wasn't aware of his father's intention that their marriage be temporary. And if she had anything at all to say about it, it wouldn't be. She was there to stay.

Chapter Nineteen

Temporary. Clara couldn't get the word out of her mind as she dressed the next morning. The day before had been long, tiring and, if she were honest with herself, fairly upsetting.

I'll show you temporary. She pulled her best day dress over her head and brushed her hair in long, strong strokes. Pulling her bonnet from the hook by the door, she stopped and turned back to the vanity.

Quickly, she fastened her mother's pearl earrings as she brushed angry tears from her cheeks. As the earrings caught the light in the mirror, she said, "Thanks, Mama. I'll need courage today."

She pulled her bonnet on, tying the strings beneath her chin when she closed the front door behind her. She set out with long strides toward her destination.

The sun had just risen, the dew sparkling on the trees and shrubs as she passed—even on the cactuses that spotted the yard.

As she reached the small, iron gate, she took a deep breath and squared her shoulders. She hesitated slightly, fleetingly wondering if this was a good idea or not.

Shaking off the thought, she opened the gate, striding into the dilapidated garden in front of the little white house.

As she pulled on a pair of worn, leather gloves and kneeled, she was startled by the buzz of a hummingbird. Mesmerized, she watched as it flew around the garden, finally hovering very close to her for a moment as the deep blue and green of its neck shimmered in the early morning light.

As quickly as it appeared, it vanished, leaving Clara with a smile.

"Thank you," she said quietly as she turned to the task at hand.

She'd never been able to have a garden of this size in Chicago and she lost herself in the pleasure of it. The pile of weeds in the far corner of the garden almost reached the top of the short, white fence when she heard the distinctive clopping of horse hooves coming up the drive.

She stood, rubbing her lower back as she bent backwards, wondering how long she'd been at it.

The horse stopped behind her and she turned slowly, looking up into the darkened face of her new father-in-law.

"What are you doing in there?" he said, his voice tight and his hand gripping the saddle horn.

"Good morning. I saw a task that needed to be done and I'm doing it. There are lovely herb plants in here under all the dead things and I thought Maria might be able to use some in the kitchen. I'd like to, too."

"Young lady, this is my wife's herb garden. No one has been allowed in here since she passed. I would appreciate it if you would leave it alone and go back to the house."

Clara sat on the short adobe fence and smoothed her apron over her skirts. She looked at the garden now with most of the weeds gone, and regarded the small starts of new plants alongside the larger ones that had been there for a while.

She reached up to her ear, fiddling with her

earring, before she stood and turned to Mr. Archer, who still glared down at her from atop his horse.

"Mr. Archer, there is great beauty here. And abundant life. New plants and new beginnings. I believe it should be tended, for everyone to see that life goes on."

He gripped the reins tighter, his knuckles turning white. His face reddened even more as he said, "This is my ranch. I am in charge here. I say what changes and what stays the same."

Clara looked down quickly, her stomach fluttering for a moment, then looked back up, meeting his gaze.

"I know you mean well, Mr. Archer, but things always change. Nothing stays the same, no matter how hard we wish it would."

The horse he was riding was unfamiliar to her, and as he gripped more tightly on the reins, it neighed loudly, rearing its head up.

He regarded her for a moment, looking quickly up to the porch as his daughters came out, staying put but watching the scene unfold before them.

"It is important that things are as they were. I

just need things to stay the same. My future is over. All I have is memories."

Clara shook her head slowly.

"But there are a lot of people here besides you. People who have dreams as well, and who are too young to have them put on hold. For things to stay the same."

"I can't. I—"

Mr. Archer's eyes flew wide open as his eldest daughter, Meg, strode past him and directly into the garden, followed by her sisters. She smiled at Clara before bending over, clearing away brown stems and leaves in a corner of the garden Clara hadn't gotten to yet.

Clara's heart swelled and soon, the garden was a flurry of activity with all the girls taking a patch as their own and adding to the pile of weeds in the corner.

Mr. Archer sat rigid in his saddle, watching in silence as his horse began to stomp and neigh louder. As Pepper, the sixth of his daughters, passed through the gate and pulled it closed behind her, he stiffened even more, his horse rearing up on its hind legs as it took off toward the stables, its rider trying to slow it without much success.

As he turned at the bottom of the road after having regained control of the horse, Meg stood, shielding her eyes against the sun and looking after her father as he became smaller on the horizon.

"We didn't dare come in here before, even though we wanted Mama's garden to be alive again." She wiped a tear away with the back of her hand.

"I know this hasn't been easy for any of you," Clara said as she wrapped her arm around her new sister-in-law's shoulder.

"Least of all for Papa. He's just not been the same," Tara said as she tugged more weeds, throwing them behind her in rapid succession.

"Well, what's going on here?" Hank said as he spotted them from the porch. "Clara, you missed breakfast. I looked for you."

He strode down the drive toward the little white house and enclosed garden, his chin falling as he saw all seven ladies turning the garden into something he hadn't seen for too long.

Clara stood, looking to where Mr. Archer had gone. "The girls and I would like the garden to be as beautiful and alive as when your mother tended to it."

Hank ran his hand over his forehead. "But Pa—"

"Trust me, Hank. It's time," she said softly as she turned and smiled at the girls busily tending to their mother's handiwork.

Hank shook his head with a small smile tugging at his lips. "Okay, if you say so. Mama would be proud, I just know it."

"Yes, she would," Sage said as she stood, holding a small cherry tomato in her hand. "Look what was underneath all the brown?"

She popped it into her mouth and the girls all smiled as they returned to vigorously cleaning out the garden.

Hank took Clara's hand and mouthed the words, "Thank you."

The butterflies Clara thought had left her returned, the warmth of his hand sending tingles straight to her heart.

"I have a horse to work before its owners come. I'll be down at the stable. Maria's saved a breakfast plate for you if you're hungry."

Clara stood and watched Hank walk down the drive and turn into the big, wide doors of the stable. She couldn't help but wonder if this was a good first step, or the beginning of the end of her stay at Archer Ranch.

Chapter Twenty

The next few days flew by as Clara and the girls tidied up the garden and Hank worked with clients in the arena.

The first day, Maria had called Clara into the kitchen after breakfast, and Clara started to roll up her sleeves, ready to help with the dishes.

Maria laughed as she turned. "No, no, Miss Clara. The girls have their assignments, and this isn't yours. I wanted to tell you that I will prepare a basket for lunch for you to take to Mr. Hank down at the arena."

Clara stopped as the older woman pulled her apron over her head and turned to the kitchen window, busying herself setting dishes in the sink.

"Hank's pretty busy. I—"

Maria turned from the window, her eyes misting as she wiped her hands on her apron. "You have brought fresh air to this heavy house. Things are changing, and no one is ever too busy for love."

Clara tugged at her sleeve and tried not to smile at Maria's vote of confidence. *Love…that would be nice.*

"Just be here at noon and I'll have it ready." She patted Clara's cheek and began to hum as she turned back to the dishes.

Each day, Maria had prepared a basket for her to take to Hank. Now, as she strode down the lane with the basket of lunch on her arm, she felt a lightness in her step. The past few days had been a nice opportunity to get to know Hank as they had lunch together and sat out in the evenings, either on the porch or the patio.

She'd made no attempt to avoid Mr. Archer, but had noticed that he kept a wide berth of her. That suited her fine. She'd said what she wanted to say and just gone about her business, hoping that she'd made something—anything—better.

She passed through the stable, stopping to stroke the noses of the horses that came up to visit her, noticing that only those on one side of the stables did.

As she glanced to her right, she noticed the

horse Mr. Archer had been riding the other day. It was quite tall and all muscle, and it hit the side of the stall with its hoof as its ears turned in her direction.

She shivered as she continued on toward the arena and rounded the corner of the stable. Hank was just waving goodbye as a father and small son walked out the gate, their horse calmly following.

She spread a tablecloth on the table under the tree and smiled as Hank walked up. He wiped his neck with a handkerchief, a sheen of sweat on his forehead and sat down on the bench.

"Thank you for this, Clara. I've come to look forward to it," he said as he helped her remove sandwiches and potato salad from the basket she'd brought.

She poured him a tin cup of tea before she sat down opposite him.

"I'm so glad you enjoy it. I sure enjoy the company," she said as they clinked their tin cups together. She enjoyed the cool tea sliding down her throat.

"I do, too," he said, his eyes gleaming as he cocked his head and regarded her.

"I thought I might find you here." Mr. Archer's voice rang out from the stables as he strode toward them.

"Yes, Father. I'm giving lessons today again," Hank said as he took a bite of his sandwich.

"Yes, I see. It would be much more helpful if you would assist in the preparations for the next cattle drive. It's imminent," he said, folding his arms over his chest.

"Pa, I know I agreed to continue…at least this last time…but I've made commitments to folks in town for training their horses. I need to finish up before I go."

"This *hobby* of yours isn't bringing anything into the ranch, Hank. We can't have it continue. Your time is best spent on the trail."

Hank sighed as he propped his elbows on the table, his head in his hands. "I'll just finish up this next week and—"

"No, you won't. You'll leave this weekend."

Hank's head snapped up and Clara's hand flew to her mouth as Mr. Archer turned his head away toward the horizon.

"Pa, you can't—"

"I can and I will. You have three days. Ben has been taking your place while you've fooled around here, getting everything ready. But you'll need to ride out with them and take charge of the horses."

"Well, hello."

All three of their heads snapped in the direction of the female voice near the stables, and Clara breathed out a big sigh of relief as Suzanne walked down to where they sat.

Her smile wide, she hugged Clara and said, "Hello, Mrs. Archer. I haven't seen you since the wedding."

Hank beamed at Clara but Mr. Archer visibly stiffened, pulling his hat further down his forehead and shoving his hands in his pockets."

"Mrs. Archer? That's…"

He turned toward the stables and strode away, leaving his thought unfinished.

"Oh, I'm sorry. Did I say something wrong?" Suzanne said, her hand on her chest and her brows raised.

"No, no," Hank said. "It's just Pa."

Clara looked down and sighed. "He's not doing well with his wife's passing."

"I see that," Suzanne said, sitting down beside her friend.

"And he's insisting I head out on the trail. This weekend," Hank added, his brow furrowed.

"Already?" Suzanne asked, her mouth falling open. "But you've only just—"

"I don't think he considers this a real marriage." Clara twisted her napkin in her hands.

"Well, it isn't, quite yet," Suzanne said. "You two are still getting to know each other."

Hank's ears reddened as he busied himself in the basket. He pulled a piece of pie out of the basket, his hand stopping mid-air as he asked Suzanne, "Did you bring the twins?"

"Yes, I did. They wanted to stop and pet Regalo for a moment, so I—"

The loud neighing of a horse followed by a bang pierced the air and Hank set out like a shot toward the stable, the massive horse that Mr. Archer usually rode almost knocking him down as it ran past, followed close behind by two more.

"Clara, open the gate to the arena. I'll find the girls," he shouted as Clara and Suzanne ran behind him.

As she ran to the gate of the arena, Clara's heart thudded in her chest, the horses rearing and neighing and running in circles all around her. She remembered what Suzanne had said, and for the first time felt frightened around them.

"They're scared but not hurt," Hank said as he ran toward her. "Suzanne's with them."

"Hey, Major, you settle down," Mr. Archer yelled as he ran down from the house toward the commotion.

Hank had moved to the opposite side of the arena, speaking to the horses as they reared and charged at one another.

"Clara, go in the stable. It's not safe here," her father-in-law shouted as he passed her and ran to help Hank.

Her heart still beating wildly, Clara backed slowly toward the stable, the cries of Lucy and Lily growing louder as she neared.

"Are you all right?" Clara said, kneeling down to Suzanne, who had both girls clasped tightly in her arms.

"We're sorry, Aunt Clara. They wanted out," Lucy wailed.

"Ssssh," Clara whispered. It's all right. It'll be fine."

She stood and moved back to the stable door, watching in awe as Hank and his father took very different approaches to trying to get the horses into the arena.

As Mr. Archer moved toward one, yelling and flailing his arms, it would move away.

Hank, flanking the other side, moved calmly, quietly, and was able to slowly usher the horse he was closest to into the arena, where it ran to the far end and settled.

As Hank and his father closed the arena gate behind the last of the horses, Hank rested his arms on the top of the fence as his father turned back toward the stable, his hands clenching as he strode up the hill.

Hank took his hat off and looked after his father, wiping his forehead with his sleeve.

"Are the girls all right?" Mr. Archer asked as he

entered the stable door and saw Suzanne, Lucy and Lily.

"I believe so, Mr. Archer. Just frightened."

"Well, good," he said gruffly as he continued through the stable and out the other door, heading up toward the house.

Chapter Twenty-One

Suzanne walked up to the main house with Clara as Hank led the final horse from the arena back to the stable. Lucy and Lily still trembled, Clara noticed, as she and Suzanne each carried one of the girls up the drive.

They set the girls down on the porch swing and Clara rushed inside to grab a pitcher of lemonade and some glasses. She opened the door, and as she set the pitcher and glasses on the table near Suzanne, Hank's boots sounded on the porch steps.

"That was mighty scary," Hank said. He took off his hat and hung it on a hook by the front door.

"It sure was," Suzanne said, each of her arms hugging one of the twins tightly to her.

Hank crouched and smoothed Lucy's hair away from her face. "What happened, girls?"

Lily grabbed her mother's waist again, her eyes

wide as she looked at Lucy.

"The horses wanted to come out and play." Lucy buried her head in Suzanne's lap as her mother stroked her hair and looked at Hank, shrugging her shoulders.

He looked down a moment, his elbows resting on his knees as he squatted, as close to eye level with the twins as he could get.

"They did, did they?" He smiled reassuringly at Lucy, who peered up at him from her mother's skirts.

"I...I think so. They were trying to get out, so I thought—"

"We didn't know, Mama. We didn't," Lily said, her eyes welling with tears again.

"I know you didn't, sweetheart. Mama shouldn't have left you alone in there, anyway." Suzanne shook her head, and looked at Clara.

"Well, how did the doors to the stalls get opened?" Hank stood and sat in a chair opposite Suzanne and the girls, his elbows on his knees as he leaned forward.

"Lucy said we should pull a crate over to be

taller, so we could reach the handles. We didn't know that the horses would be mad like that, Uncle Hank."

"No, no, you wouldn't have. But it's not safe to let any horses out when there's no grown-up around," he said, reaching forward and tugging gently at Lucy's braid with a smile.

"I'm very sorry," Lily said, looking up into her mother's eyes as she wiped away a tear with the back of her hand.

"I know you are, sweetheart." Suzanne hugged both of the girls tightly, kissing each one on top of their heads. "Mama's sorry, too, Hank."

He laughed, taking a glance at Clara. "You all right?"

Clara sat in the chair beside Hank and poured two glasses of lemonade, handing one to each of the twins.

"Yes, yes, of course. I've never seen horses behave that way, though. It was quite frightening and I'm so grateful you were there, Hank."

Hank glanced down at the stables, his face clouding. "So am I. And good Pa was there to help."

"I have to say," Suzanne said as she stole a sip of lemonade from Lucy's glass, "it sure was different, though, how the horses behaved around you and your Pa."

"What do you mean?" Hank's brow furrowed as he turned back to Suzanne.

Suzanne shifted her eyes quickly to Clara.

"Hank, the way the horses reacted to you was very different than to your father. She poured a glass of lemonade and handed it to Hank.

Hank frowned and studied the lemonade, swirling it in his glass.

"I guess I hadn't really thought of it that way. Not with horses that I haven't personally trained. And those horses on that side of the stable—none of them are horses I've had anything to do with. They're the hands' horses and waiting to go on the trail. Except for Pa's, of course."

"You really saved the day," Suzanne said. "I know that we caused the trouble, but what if you hadn't been here? To be honest, I'm not sure your father could have done that, even with one of the hands helping."

Hank sighed, gazing again back at the barn.

"I don't know about that. Everybody seems to manage well enough."

"I hate to see you go back out on the trail," Clara said quietly.

"So do I," Suzanne said, looking from Hank to Clara. "You just got—"

"We don't want you to leave, either. Do we, Lily?" Lucy sat up, poking her sister.

"No, we don't," Lily said, scowling.

Hank sighed, his lips pressed together.

He shook his head and said, "I don't want to go either. But unless I can convince Pa that it makes sense, that the cost of another hand on the drive would be okay, and I could be more valuable here, I'm afraid it's going to happen. And soon."

Clara stood and leaned against the porch railing, looking past the garden in front of the little white house that was now much more green, and onto the stables.

"Hank, how many horses have you trained here? Just this time, since you've been off the trail?" Clara asked, one eyebrow raised.

He rubbed the back of his neck, sipping from

his lemonade. "Oh, I reckon maybe ten? I'm not sure."

Suzanne perked up, her eyes wide as she looked at Clara.

"And I know of many more people who have wanted you to do it." She sat up straight on the bench, Lily and Lucy perking up beside her.

"And you mentioned that you do it as a favor. Do you know that Mrs. Beckett said she wanted to pay you, and that others did, as well?"

Clara paced the length of the porch now, her heart beating faster.

"Oh, yeah, people offer to pay. But I don't...I've never.."

"What if you did accept payment, Hank, even if just a little? Do you think there'd be enough people who'd do it to make enough money at least to hire a hand for the trail?" Clara asked, her eyes bright.

"I don't know..."

"Well, I do, Hank," Suzanne said. "Sadie said she gets asked all the time at the restaurant whether you're home and training horses or not. Guess everyone knows you and Tripp are friends.

Thought he might know."

Hank blew out a deep breath. "I guess I've just never really thought about it. You really think it might work?"

His hopefulness tugged at Clara's heart and she smiled, turning to Suzanne.

"What if we put an ad in the paper and see what response we get? That way, we can lay it all out and present it to your father. He'd have numbers to look at to consider it."

"The editor of the paper is a friend of James. If you write something up, I can take it by on the way home. Maybe he could even get it in for tomorrow," Suzanne said.

Clara turned to the door. "First, we'll need a name."

"Hang on there, ladies. Hold up a minute," Hank said, holding his hands up toward them. "This is all happening a little fast, don't you think?"

Clara and Suzanne looked at each other and burst out laughing.

"Fast? We got married in just a few days, just

like Tripp and Sadie. The restaurant went up in a week. This is just keeping in line with everything else."

Clara smiled as she opened the front door, heading to the desk and grabbing paper and pen.

"Suzanne, what do you think? You've known Pa a while." Hank pushed his dark hair back, his blue eyes watching the door for Clara.

"Hank, your Pa's not been the same since your Mama died, you know that. But the Beau Archer I knew before that happened would have thought this a grand idea." Suzanne leaned forward, patting Hank's knee.

"Not to worry. We can make it work."

Clara strode back onto the porch and sat down by Hank, tapping the quill on her chin.

"Now, all we need is a name."

"Hank's Horses?" Hank said.

Clara frowned. "No, no, not catchy enough. How about Hank's Horse Training?"

"Too simple," Suzanne said, drumming her fingers on the bench. "I know, what about Happy Horses from Hank?"

Hank laughed, his head falling into his hands. He looked up and said, "I'm not sure we're going to think of anything. They all sound silly."

"Hank's Happy Horses," Lucy chimed in and Hank laughed, clapping his hands.

"What do you think, ladies? I like that one," Hank said, clapping his hands and nodding his head slightly toward Lucy.

They all agreed, and Clara quickly wrote out an ad for Suzanne to take to the *Tombstone Epitaph*.

As Suzanne and the twins turned their buggy down the drive, Hank took Clara's hand and turned her toward him.

"I want you to know that whether or not this works out, I really appreciate you believing in me. I haven't felt like that for a long time," he said as he peered down at her, his eyes soft.

She lifted her chin up toward him and placed her hand on his cheek.

"I'm glad, Hank. Everybody needs to be believed in. Supported. Loved. It's a good thing."

He took her hand and kissed the back of it.

"Yes, I'm beginning to see that," he said as he

leaned closer to her.

Rosemary poked her head out the front door and said, "Hank, Maria asked if you'd bring up some wood for the stove so she can start supper."

They pulled away from each other and Hank cleared his throat.

"Sure. Tell her I'll bring it right up."

Clara noticed Hank's ears redden before he was able to pull his hat down over them. She smiled behind her hand.

"You know, Hank, there's really nothing to be shy about. We are married, after all."

Hank turned quickly to her, a smile spreading across his face. "Yeah, I guess we are."

He lifted his hat off, took two strides toward her and kissed her on her cheek, quick and soft. Her heart fluttered as he nodded at her and headed down to the wood pile, whistling one of his favorite tunes.

Chapter Twenty-Two

Hank laughed a few days later when Clara handed him the list of people who wanted to sign up for Hank to train their horses.

"Are you sure?" he asked Clara, his eyebrows raised in surprise.

"I'm positive. They all saw the ad or heard about it from a friend."

"This is more than I could do in a couple of months," he said as he scanned the list in his hand.

"Precisely how long you would have been on the trail." Clara smiled as she took Hank's hand and pulled him to sit beside her on the porch swing.

"And if you look at the price we put in the ad and plan it out, is that about what it'd cost to hire a wrangler for the trail for two months?"

Clara handed him the ad and watched his eyebrows rise even further, his face reddening.

He let out a slow whistle. "You put in this much? And that many people still signed up? This would pay for ten wranglers, not just one."

Clara laughed and leaned back on the swing. "Yes. Isn't it wonderful?"

"What's wonderful?" Mr. Archer said as he clomped up the stairs, wiping sweat from his forehead with his handkerchief.

Hank stood quickly at the sound of his father's voice, leaving the swing to fall back with Clara in it. He turned and handed Clara both the newspaper and client list, and as he did, she nodded to him.

"You got a minute, Pa?" He cleared his throat and motioned for his father to sit down.

Mr. Archer narrowed his eyes at his son and slowly sat in the chair Hank had indicated. "What's this all about?" he asked, looking from Hank to Clara.

Hank shoved his hands in his pockets and began to pace as his father sat back in his chair, his arms folded over his chest.

Clara took a deep breath, hoping that this would go well. Before they put the ad in the paper, they'd written out what it would take in earnings to make this work, and the numbers had come back sound. It was a good business proposition. She just hoped Mr. Archer would see it that way.

"Pa, remember when we talked a bit ago about me not going on the trail and you said it wasn't an option? We needed me to wrangle on it as the price for a head of cattle is dropping and things are changing?"

"I did. Things definitely are changing in the industry. It's been good to us for many years, but things are lean now, and I am certain that you understand what needs to be done."

"That's one of the things I wanted to talk to you about. We've known for a while that with all of the cattle coming out of Texas through Arizona into California, where all the people are going, there's not as much demand for ours.

Clara's hand went to her chest as she caught her breath. She and Hank had been so busy—but that subject hadn't come up. She'd had no idea that things were lean on Archer Ranch.

Hank nodded apologetically to Clara. "I know I didn't share that with you, Clara. Didn't want you to worry."

Mr. Archer glared at Clara. "This really is a family issue anyway, young lady. If you'll excuse us—"

"Stop right there, Pa. Clara is my wife, and agreed to marry me to help gain the property Grandpa left. And we need that."

"Yes, we do, but—"

"So, she's made sacrifices for our benefit. Surely, she's earned the right to discuss family business."

Mr. Archer's ears reddened and he looked away, toward the stable.

"Get to the point, then. We need to talk about getting ready for the trail."

"That's just it, Pa. I'm not going, and I'd really like you to approve of that decision." Hank stopped pacing and turned squarely to his father.

"Son, we've discussed this. If that's all you wanted to talk about, I'll talk with you later about the other," Mr. Archer said as he stood.

Clara jumped up, taking the two steps to Mr. Archer, who was eye to eye with Hank.

"Mr. Archer, Hank and I believe we've found a good solution for the moment. Would you just hear Hank out?"

Mr. Archer eyed his son briefly and sat back down.

"So, what is this idea of yours?"

Hank winked at Clara as he reached for the client list and held it out to his father.

"We ran an ad in the newspaper for my new business, Hank's Happy Horses. These are all the people who signed up for training services in the past two days."

Mr. Archer glanced at the list and tossed it onto the table next to him.

"That's great, son, but you helping that many people for free won't hire us another wrangler. I need that to be you."

"Mr. Archer, take a look at this." She handed the newspaper to him and watched as his eyes lit up, his eyebrows rising as he read the ad.

He let out a slow whistle, and said, "People are willing to pay this much to have you work their horses?"

Hank smiled proudly and crossed his arms over his chest, rocking forward and back on his cowboy boots.

Mr. Archer stood and walked to the far end of the porch, his hands clasped behind him.

As they waited, Hank sat down beside Clara on the porch swing, leaning back and giving her hand a quick squeeze.

His father paced a couple more times then sat back in his chair, steepling his fingers and eyeing both Hank and Clara.

Clara thought her heart would beat right out of her chest as she waited to see what he would say. She couldn't stop her knee from bouncing as she crossed her hands in her lap and waited.

"I have to say I have noticed you're the best wrangler I've ever seen. Have a way with horses I've never witnessed in any other man."

Hank blushed at the compliment and looked down at his feet, elbows on his knees as he leaned forward.

"Thanks, Pa."

"I haven't been out on the trail with you in

years, but I got a good look at it the other day when the horses got out—er, were let out, I hear."

He smiled and pushed his hat back on his head.

"Oh," Clara exclaimed. "The girls really didn't mean to—"

Mr. Archer held up his hands to stop her, his lips curving up a bit with just a hint of a smile.

"Don't worry. I understand that, but Hank sure made quick work of getting those horses calmed down or that could have been a really bad situation."

Clara sat back hard, a big whoosh of relief coming out.

"So, you're thinking that you can make as much or more than what it would cost to hire a wrangler to replace you?"

Hank sat up and looked his father in the eye.

"Yes, sir. I believe so. New folks are coming into town all the time, work horses are retired every day and people want to make sure they have safe horses that they can trust."

"And you can deliver that?"

Hank and Clara exchanged glances, and he

reached for her hand. Turning back to his father, he said, "We know we can."

"We, is it?" Mr. Archer said, smiling as he looked from Clara to Hank.

"How about this? I'll give you a week. Postpone the drive for a few days and if in a week it's happened the way you say it will, we'll make a different plan for a wrangler on the drive. How's that?"

Hank and Clara both jumped up, Hank giving his father's hand a firm shake.

"Thank you, Pa. You know I want the ranch to be a great success, but I think this is a good idea. For me *and* the ranch."

His father tipped his hat at Clara and turned to head into the house.

"Could be, son. Could be."

As his father closed the door behind him, Hank threw his hat in the air, grabbed Clara around the waist and spun her around.

"We did it!" Clara cried as her red braid flew behind her.

Hank set her down, his broad smile warming

her heart.

"Not quite yet, but it's a good start," he said as he looked down at her.

She looked up into his piercing, blue eyes, his dark hair falling on his forehead as he bent down toward her. Her heart suddenly sped up and her toes tingled as he lifted her chin up toward him.

"Would you mind if I kissed you, Mrs. Archer?" he said softly, his lips so close to hers she could feel his breath.

"I think I'd like that, Mr. Archer."

He leaned toward her and she felt his soft lips pressed to hers. As she sunk into his embrace, she knew her butterflies had found her again and even brought all their friends.

Chapter Twenty-Three

The following week's flurry of activity had Clara keeping records of appointments, so that Hank knew where he needed to be and when. She spent most of her time sitting with people, watching him work their horses and gracefully accepting payment.

Horse after horse came through the stable, Hank tirelessly working with each and every one of them.

Today was the last day of the week they'd been given, and Clara's nerves jangled a bit, even though she knew that they'd made the money they had anticipated. She even knew exactly where it was—in a cookie jar on the vanity in her bedroom.

Just the thought of maybe Hank leaving for months at a time jarred her, and they'd spent every night getting to know each other as they sat out after supper, talking about anything and everything.

Now, on this last day, Clara sat under the big oak tree with their last clients.

"I'm just so happy that things worked out this way, Mrs. Archer. Abigail is still thrilled to have her horse, and things get easier for her every day, with Hank's training."

"Oh, Mrs. Beckett, I'm glad," Clara said as she watched Hank walk the arena with Abigail.

"We were already bemoaning Hank's imminent departure, and when we saw the ad in the paper, we were overjoyed. I do remember telling you when we first met that this is what he was born to do."

Clara sighed. She flashed back to her ride down from the train station in the stagecoach and the man she'd seen on the hill just before they'd gotten into Tombstone. She remembered that his horse had come to him on its own, and her heart swelled as she now realized it had been Hank that day.

Her heart swelled at the notion that she'd seen who he was—who he truly was—before she'd even met him.

"How are things going, Mrs. Beckett?" Mr. Archer said as he came up behind them, startling

Clara.

"Oh, Mr. Archer. How lovely to see you," she said, extending her hand. "I was just telling Mrs. Archer here that we are so pleased that her husband will be offering these services. They are sorely needed here in town."

Clara turned to her father-in-law as Mrs. Beckett referred to her as Mrs. Archer, but she saw only a smile on his face as he nodded to the lady, and then to her.

"Yes, so I've been told," he said softly.

Hank led the horse and Abigail into the stables, and Clara and Mrs. Beckett turned to follow.

Mr. Archer headed to the house. "Clara, would you and Hank come see me, please, up at the house when you've finished?"

"Of course. Shouldn't be too long."

Mrs. Beckett said, "He seems to be in better humor today than the last time we spoke."

Now that she thought of it, Clara hadn't seen Mr. Archer but at supper the entire week they'd been running Hank's new business. They'd been so busy she hadn't even known where he'd been.

Hank and Clara waved goodbye to Mrs. Beckett and Abigail as they pulled through the gates of Archer Ranch.

"Well, did we do it?" Hank asked as he wrapped his arm around Clara's shoulder and squeezed.

She reached up to grab his hand on her shoulder and held up the money Mrs. Beckett had just given her, her grin ear to ear.

"With this, we've made enough to pay for the wrangler for the whole time. Anything we make from now on out is extra."

Hank breathed a sigh of relief but was silent as they walked up the drive to the big house, arm in arm.

As they drew closer to the house, he said, "I just hope that he was serious, and won't change his mind. I love what I'm doing now, but more importantly, I couldn't bear to leave you now, Clara."

He stopped at the bottom of the porch steps and turned her to him.

"Hank, I—"

"Shhh," he said, putting his finger to her lips. "I need to finish what I was going to say."

Heat flooded her cheeks and she looked down, straightening her skirts.

He reached for her, and as he held her in his arms, he said, "I want you to know that whatever happens tonight with Pa, I will find a way to make this right. You're my wife, and I want to stay with you."

"Oh, Hank. You don't need to say that. I understand it was all for the property."

"Clara Archer," Hank said, pulling her in closer. "It may have started out that way, but I have come to realize that it was the luckiest thing that's ever happened to me."

"You have?" she said, her eyes twinkling as she looked up at him.

"Yes. And I also have realized that I love you."

Clara gasped, unable to speak as her heart had leapt in her throat. She took a deep breath and calmed down enough to say, "And I love you."

Hank leaned in to kiss her, his eyes searching her face.

"Oh, yuck," Pepper said as the front door opened and all the girls came out, followed by their father.

"Now, girls, that's what people in love do. Later. When they're grown up. And married," Mr. Archer said, smiling but wringing his hands as he surveyed his six daughters who would all eventually be of marrying age. And actually, some already were.

Hank laughed, pulling away from Clara but holding her hand in his. "I think you're going to have a run for your money, Pa, but I'll help all I can."

His father sighed as he walked down the porch stairs.

"I think I'm going to need all the help I can get," he said, stopping in front of Hank and Clara, the girls watching from the porch.

"I'll help too, Mr. Archer." Clara smiled, looking at the beautiful young ladies lined up on the porch and wondering how that would all go.

"Well, Pa, I'm sure you're wondering about—"

"Actually, I'm not wondering at all. It's pretty plain that this week has been a great success.

Hank's Happy Horses is off to a rousing good start."

"Oh, Pa," Hank said as he smiled and extended his hand to his father.

"I'm very proud of you, son." Mr. Archer took Hank's hand but pulled him into a hug, clapping him loudly on his back.

Clara tried to hide her smile behind her hand as all six of the girls burst into applause from the porch, their laughter and smiles infectious.

"You girls stop that. Let's go show Hank and Clara what we've done for them."

Shrieks of laughter led Hank and Clara to follow Mr. Archer and Hank's sisters down the lane. The girls ran ahead and stopped in front of the gate to the little white house Clara had admired since she'd arrived at Archer Ranch.

The girls stepped aside as their father approached and opened the gate, gesturing for Hank and Clara to go inside.

Hank stopped when he got to the front door.

"What is it, Pa? Is everything all right?"

"Hank and Clara, this place has been closed up

and silent for way too long. We all miss Mama, but we have to live life, and it is my hope that you are as happy as Mama and I were."

"Thank you, Mr. Archer," Clara said, resting her hand on Hank's arm.

Mr. Archer smiled and nodded at Clara.

"So, the girls and I thought you two might be desiring a little privacy, so we've spent the week while you've been working on a project."

Titters spread amongst the girls, and Meg said, "Go on, Clara, open the door."

Clara looked at the girls behind her and then to Mr. Archer, who nodded to her and gestured toward the door.

With one last look at Hank as he shrugged, she entered the small white house.

Clara stopped short as she stepped over the threshold, stock still until she felt Hank's hand on her back, gently inching her forward.

She walked slowly around the room. The shining wood floor reflected warm sunlight from the sparkling windows. She held her hand up to touch beautiful curtains spotted with prints of colorful flowers. She peeked through a doorway into a bedroom and blushed when she saw a large bed, overlaid with a lovely quilt.

The small kitchen was charming, and she finally stopped by a small dining table with a vase of daisies set in the middle.

She looked up toward Saffron, who turned crimson, her long eyelashes cast downward.

"Are these daisies from you?" Clara said to Saffron.

"Yes, they are. I want you to be happy here. I want you to stay."

"We all do," Mr. Archer said. "We've spent a lot of time here this week, remembering Mama and cleaning it up for you two. There was a fair amount of dust."

He cleared his throat as he looked at his eldest daughter, Meg, as she laughed.

"That's an understatement. It hadn't been opened in years."

"But it was fun," Sage said. "We got to pack up Mama's things and kind of say goodbye. And we want you to have a place of your own to start off your family," she said as she walked over to Clara and hugged her.

Hank looked from his father to his sisters. He strode to the girls, hugging each one of them as he said, "I just don't know how to thank you all. This is wonderful."

As he got to his father, he stopped and looked his father in the eyes for a long moment.

Mr. Archer looked down at his boots and said, "I want you and Clara to be happy, son. Like me and your mama. And we were very happy."

Hank pulled his father into a hug as Clara's eyes misted.

Maria poked her head in the door and said, "Supper is ready, everybody. Come on up when you're finished." She winked at Clara and headed back up to the house.

The girls ran behind Maria and Mr. Archer said, "I never thought all this would turn out so..."

"Wonderful?" Hank said, his eyes on Clara.

Mr. Archer laughed. "Yes, I guess that is the word. Wonderful. I'll see you two up for supper."

Clara sighed as she and Hank walked out into

the front garden and Hank closed the door behind him.

"It really is wonderful, Hank. All of it."

"It is. And so I suppose that tonight will be our real wedding night."

He laughed and grabbed her hand, pulling her to the gate as she blushed.

Before she passed through, she turned and looked at the garden they'd cleaned out when she first got there. It didn't look anything like it had in the beginning, and she grinned with pride that the flowers and herbs were coming back to life. Slowly, but they were all definitely sprouting, ready to bloom again. Just like her new family.

Epilogue

"What do you think could be so important that we were asked to go to the Occidental tonight?" Clara asked Hank as he drove the buggy out the gate of Archer Ranch.

Hank shook his head as he held the reins in one hand and put his arm around Clara, sliding her closer to him on the bench seat.

"I'm not sure. Pa just got back from his business trip and asked if we'd join him. But it'll be nice to be with everybody. Suzanne said she and the girls and James and Sadie would be there for dinner."

"Oh, wonderful. We'll get to see them all. We haven't been out in so long."

"How long has it been since we've seen anybody but Suzanne and the twins when they come to ride?"

Clara tapped her chin as she thought, her eyes

narrowed. "Well, we've been married about two months now, and I think honestly I haven't seen Tripp and Sadie but maybe once or twice since the wedding."

"Good, then it's high time we took a break from the business to have some fun."

As they pulled up to the Occidental and Hank tied the buggy to the post out front, Clara smiled as Mr. Archer came out of the restaurant, reaching his hand up to help her out.

"Well, hello. It's nice to see you." Clara said as she stepped down to the porch.

"Yes, it's nice to see you, too, Mrs. Archer."

Clara's heart tugged at his greeting. They hadn't had a chance, really, to talk about much as he'd been on business trips for much of the time they'd been married. The ranching industry was changing, and everyone at the Archer Ranch was anxious to see how things might be different.

"Thank you, Mr. Archer."

Hank's father cleared his throat. "Clara, do you remember long ago, that I asked you to call me Beau?"

"Oh, yes, I suppose I do. But I—"

He held up his hands to stop her as Hank joined them.

"No buts, please. I insist."

She tugged on her mother's pearl earring as she looked at Hank, who smiled and nodded at her.

"Well, thank you, Beau. I appreciate that."

"Thanks, Pa. It's nice to have you back," Hank said as he shook his father's hand.

"Nice to be back, son. Thanks for agreeing to join me tonight. I hear beef stew's on the menu."

Beau held his arm out for Clara, and she took it, her eyebrows raised with a smile to Hank, who followed behind them as they entered the Occidental.

"Over here," Sadie called as soon as they entered, gesturing to the small, private dining room where they'd had their wedding reception. Clara smiled as she remembered smearing Hank's face with chocolate.

Hank took Clara's wrap and bonnet as they walked into a party already in progress. James, the twins, Suzanne, Sadie and Tripp all laughed and talked. Clara's stomach rumbled as she eyed the mouth-watering buffet of appetizers lining the far wall.

Tripp nodded to Hank, Clara and Beau and tapped his glass with his fork as he cleared his throat.

He held his hand out for Sadie to join him, and Clara wondered at the color or her cheeks—bright scarlet.

"Thank you for joining us today. It's a special occasion and we wanted to share it with our family."

He smiled at Sadie as he squeezed her hand. "You'll notice soon enough, but Sadie and I—well, Sadie is with child. Maybe two," he said as he glanced at the three sets of twins in the room and laughed.

Sadie poked her elbow into his side and looked at her shoes. "I hope not, but we're very happy."

Pepper, Lucy and Lily all squealed and joined the room in laughter as they ran to hug Sadie.

"Oh, my," Suzanne said to Clara as she waited her turn to hug the mother-to-be. "And so it begins."

"Clara, Hank, it's so nice to see you. It's been a long time," Sadie said as she hugged Clara. "How is married life treating you?"

Clara thought her face would stay permanently pink at this rate. "Wonderful. I'm very happy."

Hank put his arm around her and gave her a quick squeeze. "So am I."

"Congratulations, Sadie, on the news. We're so happy for you," Clara said as Sadie beamed at Tripp.

"I told you you two were meant for each other," Suzanne said as she hugged Clara, too. "I love when things work out like this."

"Well, maybe you can help me, then." Samuel Ford, the bartender, came through the door, his face ashen.

"Sam, what is it?" Sadie said as she rushed to him. "Here, sit down." She pulled him to one of the chairs and sat him down.

"I...I just received a letter from my mother. She's coming to visit. " He looked down at the paper in his hands, folding it and re-opening it.

"Oh, that's nice. She lives in New York, doesn't

she? I don't think I've met her yet. How lovely of her to visit," Sadie said, patting him on the shoulder as Tripp came up.

"Uh, your mother? The wealthy lady from back east? The reason you moved away?" His lips tugged up into a grin. "The one who wanted you to be a—"

"Yes, anything she deems successful. One and the same," Sam said as he rubbed his forehead.

"You don't seem happy about it," Suzanne said, her eyebrows raised.

"You don't understand. I...my mother had very firm plans for me. To be a doctor or a successful businessman, to be married with a family."

Sadie reached out and put her hand on his shoulder. "I'm sure she'll be very proud of you, Sam. There's no shame in being a bartender."

"Oh, I don't think there is. I think I'm the best bartender around, and I love what I do," Sam said. "But there's a little problem."

"Oh?" Suzanne asked.

Tripp's grin turned into a laugh. "You didn't."

Sam shook his head slowly. "Yes, I did. I told

her I was married and owned a business. I never thought she'd come this far west. She hates to be out of the city."

Suzanne's eyes twinkled as she said, "I'll be right back."

"How long do you have until she gets here?" James asked.

"Not too long, I don't think. Oh, what a disaster."

"I knew there was a reason I'd need this," Suzanne said as she came back in the room waving a copy of the *Groom's Gazette*. "Sadie and I are fresh out of friends, but look at this. We can advertise for a mail-order bride for you."

Sam's face had been ashen before, and now he turned completely white, the blood draining from his face. "I don't think I can do that."

"Sure you can," Sadie said, flipping through the flyer. "We'll figure it out tomorrow."

"Boy, this is going to be interesting," Hank said as he laughed and clapped his friend on the back.

"It's not funny. You don't know my mother," Sam said.

"You're right. It's not funny." Tripp folded his arms across his chest. "It's absolutely hilarious."

Sam shook his head, joining in the laughter surrounding him and his problem.

"Do you have one of those for husbands?" Beau asked, his eyes twinkling. "I've got a houseful of girls who are going to need one pretty soon."

"I have a feeling they're going to want to have quite a bit of say in that." Clara reached out her hand to Hank.

"Yes, I'm sure they will. Especially now that..."

Beau pulled on his chin and looked down at his boots.

"Pa? You all right?" Hank asked.

"Yes, son. There's just something I've been meaning to say, and not sure of the right words."

Hank put his arm around Clara and waited. Clara smoothed her skirts as she watched Beau gain his courage.

"I mostly just wanted to thank the two of you. You, Hank, for having the good luck to choose a special lady like Clara, here."

Hank laughed and said, "Don't I know it.

Luckiest day of my life."

Clara's ears burned at the compliment.

"And to thank you, Clara, for everything you've done for me, Hank and the girls. I never realized until you came that we were all holding our breath, not grieving Katie and moving on."

"Oh, Mr.—Beau," Clara said as she placed her hand on his shoulder. "I don't believe I did much, but I can't tell you how happy I am that things are better…lighter around Archer Ranch."

Beau tilted his head up toward her. "We're all glad. And grateful. Maria, too. Says she doesn't have to tiptoe around us anymore."

Hank smiled. "I must say that's a nice change."

"I have to agree with you, son. Everything's changed. For the better, I might add," Beau said as he lifted his glass to Clara.

"Thank you for choosing me, Hank." Clara smiled as she looked around the room. "I'm so grateful for my new family. All of them.

THE END

CINDY CALDWELL

ABOUT THE AUTHOR

Cindy Caldwell has wanted to write books since she was a little girl, reading under the covers with a flashlight because she wanted to know what happened next. Her father's favorites, Louis L'amour and Max Brand, inspired these Wild West Frontier Brides stories, and she's honored to have you as a reader.

Made in the USA
Middletown, DE
22 October 2015